A Tale of t,~ ~~~

Might & Magic

BY LEE M. COOPER

This is a work of fiction. Names, characters, businesses, places, events, and incidents are either the products of the author's imagination or used in a fictitious manner. Any resemblance to actual persons, living or dead, or actual events is purely coincidental.

All rights reserved. No part of this book may be reproduced or used in any manner without the prior written permission of the copyright owner, except for the use of brief quotations in a book review.

Copyright © 2024 by Lee M. Cooper

BY LEE M. COOPER

Contents

Chapter 1: Humble Beginnings 2

Chapter 2: The KingsGuard 10

Chapter 3: Might & Magic 18

Chapter 4: In the service of a King 26

Chapter 5: An Emperor of Legend 38

Chapter 6: Reckoning 48

Chapter 7: Force of Nature 63

Chapter 8: A Lost Hope 79

Chapter 9: Knightfall 89

Chapter 10: Revelation 102

Chapter 11: Round One 110

Chapter 12: Round Two 119

Chapter 13: Shroud of Darkness 128

Chapter 14: The Course of Justice 143

Chapter 15: Thunderous Pursuit 156

Chapter 16: Battle of The Ancients 173

Chapter 17: The Final Stand 190

Epilogue 202

Might & Magic

Chapter 1: Humble Beginnings

Thump, thump, thump!
Martha banged on the door.
'Max! They're here!' she shouted excitedly.
'Just a second!' he replied.

Max took a deep breath as he looked at himself in the mirror upstairs. He knew this was the biggest day of his life. Max was a young man, eighteen or so in age, of medium build and around five foot eight with short dark

BY LEE M. COOPER

hair, neatly styled back. He had a faint stubble, but otherwise was very clean cut in his appearance. He turned, straightened up, exhaled, and walked out the bathroom door and promptly down the stairs. He was greeted by his mother standing with three military dressed soldiers in the living room.

'Max, this is lieutenant…oh…apologies my memory is terrible these days ha ha' she smiled and nervously chuckled at the gentleman.

'Lieutenant mage Jaru, aghm' the tallest man said, clearing his throat.

He stepped forward towards Max looking him up and down and then once again back up and into his eyes. Max stood to attention also observing the soldiers before him, taking mental notes. They were all clad in smooth grand looking armour, graphite in colour with soft, expensive looking robes underneath. The steel plates of their armour glistened in the light of the room, they were pristinely clean, and the chest plates branched out into smooth curved edges at the shoulders. The waist and upper legs were also encased in graphite coloured matching, albeit softer, looking armour. Decorated in various military and ancient emblems that seemed somewhat foreign to Max, except for the military's recognisable crest.

Their boots were more of a hardened mahogany brown leather, which were designed to almost intertwine with where the upper leg armour met at the knee. As Max returned a sharp stare back into Jaru's eyes he also noticed they had no helmets or protective headwear of

Might & Magic

any kind on, which was an unusual site for Imperials around the city, but not completely uncommon.

Jaru, had a short dark brown beard with whisps of grey in it, a hard look in his hazel eyes and with a slight grimace on his face. However, he had long dark hair that shined startingly bright by comparison, which was braided down his back finishing just above his waist in a ponytail. He bore no visible scars but looked very battle hardened in his face.

'So today is the start of your new life, young master Starheart' Jaru said.

'I hope so Sir' Max replied, with a slight nervous smile on one side of his face.

'Well come along then, we have a shuttle waiting outside for you and best not to keep the academy waiting, oh how they do dislike late sprogs heh heh' Jaru chuckled. 'I'll give you a minute to say your goodbyes,' as he walked out the door.

'Just a minute mind you...,' he turned his head slightly to say at the door, before stepping outside and closing it behind him.

Max looked at his mum, they smiled back at one another before embracing. As her eyes welled up, his mother looked back at him.

'Remember I'm always here, don't be a stranger, make friends as best you can and don't forget......you've made me and your father very proud, even if he's no longer here to tell you himself' she muttered wiping her cheek dry.

Max replied, 'I know mum and don't worry about me, I'm tougher than I look.'

BY LEE M. COOPER

At that moment he turned, opened the door and without looking back, exited the house, closing the door confidently behind him.

A sudden gust of warm air was immediately all around him, as lieutenant Jaru and his two-security guard's stood waiting for him next to an imperial shuttle craft. It bore the same graphite colour as the soldiers' armour as it hovered in the air; the rear jets emitted a green mist like aura which kept the craft airborne. Also, along the side of the craft, was displayed the military's crest of arms, which was a very familiar sight in Max's life. He flashed back for a second in his mind, remembering fond, crystal-clear memories of his father's armour when he returned off duty, which displayed the same crest. This was the first time he had been face to face with an official military craft and was in awe of it as his eyes widened and a smile appeared across his face, like a child who had finally acquired the toy he had always wanted.

'Let's be off young master Starheart...' Jaru barked as the two soldiers flanking him hopped aboard.

Max adjusted the bag he was carrying over his shoulder and ran to jump on board as well. Jaru was the last to board as he took his seat, strapped himself in and shouted to the pilot.

'Let's go.'

With that, the pilot immediately began to climb into the bright, clear blue sky towards the Imperial academy.

From this high up view over the imperial capital city of Kavlos, Max could see the middle-class working area where his house was located to the East of the city. The

Might & Magic

area was very flat, with many small buildings all similar in structure and quite bland looking to the eye from afar.

To the West, lay the upper-class region of the city where primarily the wealthiest of the city's population dwelt. This was mostly comprised of tall glass like buildings, which reached upwards from the earth, high towards the sky and glistened like jewels in the morning sun's rays of light.

In the southern region lay the city's gates, this was more of a military post that was operated with exact precision. Kavlos was a very populous city, the capital of the planet Omeria and where thousands of outsiders and citizens alike were coming and going every day about their ordinary lives. Exact documentation was always required, stating purpose of visit, background, occupation, and various other personal details, as was set down by the King himself and thus enforced with an iron clad like grip.

The centre of the city mostly consisted of markets and merchants, some shady in nature and selling illegal items & trinkets whereas others were very reputable and sold items & wares of only the highest quality. The city itself was also famous for the gigantic magic field which encased the city like a bubble. It was clear in colour and emitted from the emperor's grand citadel itself in the distant north of the city and touched all the way down to just outside the city's perimeter.

This was designed & used as a protective measure from outside attack, which very rarely ever happened. As the shuttle banked and headed north towards its destination, Max could now see a close-up of the city's famous Imperial academy of Sorcery. It lay behind a gigantic wall of stone that cut along the northernmost part of the city, distinguishing it from the rest of the residential areas. It was here, in this temple, where so many began their training in the mystic arts.

The great wall was raised up on a mountainside and as they climbed above and beyond the great wall and the academy temple, there stood the great royal tower of Kavlos where the King himself resided. The tower itself was a great graphite spire (a deliberate colour tone in line with that of the imperial code), smooth and circular; it was in shape with great diamonds encrusted around the circumference of the tower's peak. This tower was encircled by a greater yet smaller, castle-like structure. Naturally, this was heavily guarded and blanketed by military personnel, vehicles, and armaments as far as the eye could see. Only by appointment of the King himself, would anyone be admitted entry here.

And beyond that, protruding from the highest part of the mountain lay the great citadel of the emperor. Never has a grander structure been seen anywhere else on Omeria. The topmost peak of the citadel itself, lay in line with the summit of the magnificent mountain it was built into. The protective magic field obviously also originated from here, the citadel itself was white in colour and stood out from all else in Kavlos, able to be seen from anywhere in the city and far beyond.

The only way into this great citadel was from a private mountainside path from behind the Kings tower, or via an air shuttle privately used by the King himself.

As Max was soaking all of this in, he was suddenly met with dozens of similar aircraft all spiralling in precision-like

Might & Magic

unison throughout the upper mountainous regions. He could feel his shuttle begin descending slowly behind the great wall & towards the entrance of the academy temple as it began rotating into its allotted parking bay.

'Ok, everybody off, Max Starheart...follow me' Jaru said.

As they stepped off the shuttle, Jaru led Max towards the huge doors of the academy temple. From here, everyone stood outside, lined up neatly and were patrolled by various soldiers, sergeants, and other military ranked personnel. Hundreds of new recruits suddenly littered the academy's approach. Most were in their late teens and early twenties all with excited looks on their faces at the prospect of serving the world's foremost royalty and most powerful military power in existence.

Jaru guided Max to a spot amongst the lines of promptly gathered new recruits and then parted with his final words.

'Master Starheart, please wait here. From here on out, I must bid you farewell, but I hope our paths meet again someday. I'll be watching, good luck.'

Max nodded his head in acknowledgment and spoke

'Thank you, sir. As do I also.'

Jaru smiled, then turned to position himself into a strict military stance with his back straight, eyes forward and head held high.

At that moment, a loud Gonging noise could suddenly be heard, followed by soldiers shouting.

'All new recruits in line for inspection!'

As if in unison, all the young, smiling faces suddenly turned very serious, and all sound fell silent. The recruits were lined immaculately, facing forwards. At that moment, a loud creaking could be heard from the academy's huge ominous doors as they began to slowly break open.

A huge green, ghoulish like glow came from within, as soldiers all clad in their dark coloured imperial armour came storming out to form ranks in front of the battalions of new recruits and then suddenly, three outlines appeared out from the green glow within...

Might & Magic

Chapter 2: The KingsGuard

Max squinted as he tried to make out who or what was in front of him, beyond the sudden present bright green light. He could make out three what seemed like very profound looking figures stood motionless. Three perfectly

BY LEE M. COOPER

lined silhouettes that stood side by side, draped in darkness and mystery. Gasps and low chatter could be heard amongst the ranks of new recruits as they too looked on in awe, the three figures then began to walk through the grand gateway of the imperial academy and down the marble stairs that followed.

'Wait a minute' Max thought to himself, as he was trying to piece together in his mind who these three could possibly be, he remembered he had heard about a 'KingsGuard' from his father years ago, and the imperial manuscripts he'd read before.

'Could it really be them?! Would they really come to see us here now?!' He thought to himself. As the figures arrived at the bottom of the stairs, they could each now be seen clearly stood in front of the recruits. From left to right they each stepped forward, introducing themselves.

'If we may have your attention, please. Before you, stand The KingsGuard, the very same you may have read and heard about' said the first man.

The man was tall, around six feet with long silver hair that draped down his back and over his shoulders. He was clean shaven, of slender build but had a powerful presence about him. He stood proudly with his shoulders back in a confident manner. His armour was like that worn by the upper-class imperial personnel only with a much grander design.

The patterns and insignias resembled curling serpent like bodies wrapped all around from the bottom of his armoured boots to his shoulders and culminating across his chest, in which lay a fiery & menacing ancient dragon

Might & Magic

like design not like anything seen in this world for many centuries. The colour was also different, a deep red which only further accentuated his burning amber, otherworldly eyes. All three of the KingsGuard had long, exquisite looking cloaks that began at the rear shoulder plates that flowed down their backs, finishing just before it touched the ground. They only helped further to impart their already clear significance.

'I am Thamir, we are the King's personal guard and through us flows his every command, his every wish' as he looked around in a cautious like manner.

'And have no doubt about it we will see it done. And no less will be expected from all of you stood here today.'

After a brief pause the second man to his right also took a step forward and crossed his arms in a very commanding gesture.

'You may call me, Onix.' He declared.

'We are here to oversee your training, as commanded by our great King. There is much you will not understand over the coming days and months however be assured; time is a great mentor.'

Onix was around matching height to Thamir, his dark green eyes stood out and gave off a glint of mystery & power. His armour was also much grander looking, but he was clad in a dark forest green shade. He had short feathery like dark hair and a medium length full beard which finished just above his chest in a braid, decorated with golden beads of ancient foreign looking design. His outfit too, was spectacular. But this time instead of a serpent & dragon pattern, his was that of majestic mountains and leaf like shapes all over. It was clear to Max

BY LEE M. COOPER

that this individual, was more attuned to nature & the land from a physical standpoint.

"We are the oldest living sorcerers now left in this world. We have seen countless serve our illustrious King and his emperor, for that, is an honour we hope you too will share in time. Our presence here is to help guide you and oversee your training that lies ahead… for you will need it in the troublesome times to come.'

Max and the other recruits looked at each other with now confused and slightly worried frowns upon their faces.

Then the third and final stepped forward, placing his hands on his hips as he quietly looked around, surveying the young men & women in front of him. This KingsGuard presented himself also very proudly, if but a little more sternly looking than his fellow peers. His entire body clad in a brilliant blue with ancient scriptures covering of storms and lightning bolts. Matching their height, he fashioned a scar which reached from over his top right brow across his face and ended just below his left cheek. His eyes illuminated with a crackling blue hue & were visibly brimming with power, not that of a normal human by any means. He had medium length wavey blonde hair, tied up into a knot.

'Kain is my name and to reiterate the words that my brothers have imparted on you already, these are indeed uncertain times when powers from foreign lands have begun to stir, this much we have felt.'

He Continued.

Might & Magic

'Although Kavlos is the strongest power in all of Omeria and has been since days of old, there is always an ever-present great evil and ambition from those elsewhere, who would seek to subdue our Emperor and King and take Kavlos as their own.'

Thamir then interrupted 'It is you who are the future of this great city, and it is all our duties to see it protected. Our emperor is wise and just and we must continue to follow his guidance' he remarked.

Onix then abruptly proclaimed

'For Kavlos!'

A notion that could be heard echoing throughout the academy grounds.

Then the three took a slight bow crossing one arm across their chests in an almost ritualistic fashion.

At that moment, the three raised their heads, turned, and began to walk across the academy's outer entrance boarding a shuttle which was waiting for them nearby as Max and his fellow recruits looked on. It then took off with immediate haste and launched off high into the sky, banking back over the academy temple and towards the King's palace. Max had to remind himself to close his mouth and not to look so dumb to the others, he could not believe what he just experienced, however.

'That was unreal....and scary as hell!' he thought.

There was more shouting that followed, as the sergeants gathered the recruits into single file lines that followed into the great doors of the academy. The green ghoulish like glow still emanated as Max and the others approached the threshold, but he could now see this was from two gigantic braziers that were lit from just within. Whatever

BY LEE M. COOPER

magic was conjured to light these ancient looking torches, must have been powerful indeed, as Max reflected.

The recruits were guided down an inner stairwell not far inside the upper hall, which reached deep into the mountain that the academies temple was carved into. When Max and the others eventually reached the bottom of the seemingly never ending, eerily lit stairwell, a gigantic grand hall lay before them. Great pillars of marble laced with gold could be seen throughout, reaching fifty or sixty feet tall as far as the eye could see. This had clearly been here for a long, long time and the enormity of the hall was unlike anything any of the recruits had ever seen before. Still the green ghostly hue could be seen lit throughout, which was a mainstay of the school.

Beautifully carved into the recesses of the walls were grand oak doors spaced around fifteen to twenty feet apart, each clearly expensive looking and numbered down towards the end of the hall.

'Alright listen up, you have arrived at your barracks which will be your new quarters between lessons' one of the sergeants said.

'You will be given a number in accordance with your house surname, and this will direct you to where you need to be. Please be quick, please be orderly and please get a good night's rest, you will need it for tomorrow.'

'Number thirty-four hmmm looks like it's on the left side' as Max shuffled along, glancing downwards and forwards between his handed papers and the numbers along the wall. As he walked up to the door, a number of recruits were already slowly piling in. Inside, the room quarters

Might & Magic

were separated by two corridors, one to the left, one to the right both male and female indicated.

As Max turned left towards the male dormitory and followed the short corridor down into the room where he would be staying, he heard a familiar voice. 'Well well, well, I was wondering when I'd see you here, buddy...' The voice came from a young man around twenty, well built, and he clearly paid attention to his presentation by the look of how his dark blonde locks were neatly combed back. His short blonde beard was very well manicured too. And his uniform was exceptionally clean, pressed to perfection.

'Jarrel? Jarrel Jones?' Max amusingly grumbled with a smirk on his face as he looked around the corner.

'The one and only pal, I'm just glad they put us together, thought they might with our father's military background an all' he confidently said.

'And let's face it, you need me to keep you sharp' he said with a wink and a grin.

Max replied 'Yeah, yeah, ok, ok. You keep thinking that mate. Just because our dads were old war buddies and we grew up together, don't go thinking we have to follow suit ya know. You're a bad influence, how many times have you gotten me into trouble? As soon as I'm ready to graduate, I'm out of here and to the front lines. So don't miss me, will ya?' he laughed.

'Oh Max, what makes you think you will be leaving me behind? You know since an early age I can do things few others have ever been able to do at our ages' Jarrel said.

BY LEE M. COOPER

'And what's more, I've no doubt that I will stand head and shoulders above the rest of these noobs,' Jarrel whispered into his ear.

Max laughed to himself and placed his hand on Jarrel's shoulder.

'Whatever mate, ever Mr confident eh. I suppose I'm glad to see you here too. I can laugh when I beat your class scores not to mention this will be the real proof of who is the better man, I guess huh.'

With that last remark, Max walked across the room to an empty bed and started to unpack his bag with a grin, as Jarrel shook his head with a smile, turned around and did the same.

Might & Magic

Chapter 3: Might & Magic

The next morning, Max attended his first academy history lesson. The room lay not too far from his quarters further along in the great hall. He arrived promptly, full of excitement. Not only for his first real lesson of any kind, but also because he was fascinated by the world around him. The royal family, where magic originated from in their world, even to possibly learn more about the

BY LEE M. COOPER

disappearance of his father, who served so many years ago. He had always been like a sponge, for wanting to absorb all the knowledge he could.

As he took his seat at one of the desks in the classroom, a man entered the room at the front through a small side door. He looked young, around twenty-seven, maybe twenty-eight. Much too young to be teaching a history class, Max pondered. He had a kind smile and a way about him, his calm movement and relaxed demeanour, as he began to speak to the class.

'My name is instructor Hau, Chi Hau and I will be your Magical arts & Imperial History tutor' he said. 'I am here to put to bed any falsehoods you may have heard, any legends, myths, or rumours that your friends and family might have misled you with. I am here to help explain what is real, what can be accomplished and to help you understand exactly what kind of force you will be fighting for.'

'Let us start at the beginning' he started. 'Since the dawn of time, Omeria has evolved and its people along with it. Our planet is centuries old as we know and we have grown from mere specs of life, into the more technological advancements you see around you today. But one thing we have always known from the days of old ....is that what we call 'magic.'

Chi was visibly a very animated instructor, the kind of man who seemed excitable every time he taught his class, no matter if he had said the same thing once or a thousand times over.

Might & Magic

'Since ancient times, Kavlos has held a royal family, and that family has ruled for a millennium mostly in peace and prosperity. They have managed to do this with combined might and magic......in modern terms....us! Now yesterday, you met the KingsGuard. This is a very rare honour indeed; they are usually leading our forces throughout the world or are carrying out our great King's commands personally. The 'Kings Fist' as they are also known, are of the most ancient & prolific order of sorcerers Omeria has ever known. They have served numerous kings over the years and though admittedly not much is known about them, even to us now, what we do know is that they were trained and commanded to protect the King at all costs by the emperor himself.'

The students all sat silently taking in the information, looks of wonder upon their faces. One of the recruits then chimed in.

'Sir, you say they are ancient sorcerer's sir, but how can they have lived for hundreds and hundreds of years? And what can you tell us of the emperor. I know a lot of us here are eager to learn more about him, he is such a mysterious character.'

'Ah yes, all in good time young man,' he replied with a smile. 'What I can tell you is that the King's Fist have survived for so many years BECAUSE they have learnt and mastered the great magic of the elements. This in turn has also empowered them to keep their youth amongst many other.... shall we say unexplainable feats. To me and you they appear no more than to be in their late thirties or early forties but this...THIS is the power that we can endeavour to learn and evolve with!' he excitedly remarked.

'Of course, that is should they eventually see us as worthy of learning this power.'

Jarrel who was also in the class then asked, 'so why have we not been able to pass on this knowledge of de-aging or whatever they have learnt, to the masses sir?'

Chi turned to him and thoughtfully replied.

'That is exactly why we cannot. If the entire world had that kind of power, then it would fall into madness and chaos. The KingsGuard were very intricate & careful in what they passed along to others, and they know that they have a responsibility to the emperor to ultimately safeguard this power. Now you may have noticed from their appearances that this reflects what their powers are a derivative of.

For example, Thamir is capable of conjuring powerful fire magic, rain meteors from the sky should he deem it fit and legend tells, he was even able to summon the ancient dragon beasts of old, but that...was......many a century ago and possibly just a legend as I say ha ha' Chi chuckled to himself but still with a look of wonder about him.

He continued 'Onix has the ability to use the earth and the more natural aspects of the land and bend it to his whim. He has been known to grow great lavish forests and breed animal life into areas that were otherwise barren or desert like once before. He may even be so powerful as to be able to shake the very mountain Kavlos is built upon .... but let us hope he does not,' he muttered in a shaken tone.

Might & Magic

'That then brings us to Kain, he has been gifted with control of the weather itself, to be able to control it and conjure great storms which have been a mighty blessing in the various campaigns of the past.'

At that point, a young girl raised her hand and asked, 'if they are so powerful, then why do they help the emperor, why not overthrow him or use this powerful magic to meet their own ends?'

'A good question young lady, and the answer has a purpose' Chi Hau said.

'The emperor is said to be more powerful than all three of these high mages and not only that. The mages, they are also very attuned to our planet in ways we cannot hope to fathom. We need them to help keep the balance of nature afloat. Which of course, I know sounds ridiculous' he laughed.

'Now open your books to page one' Chi Hau said, as the flipping of pages echoed throughout the class.

The next day at lunch, Jarrel walked over to where Max was sitting eating, at a small table in the corner of the cafeteria.

'So, you buying that story about the KingsGuard from Instructor Hau yesterday? I know the mystic arts themselves are an incredible thing and all but being able to live centuries and all that emperor mumbo jumbo......I mean c'mon, does he even really exist?! No one's supposedly ever seen him. I think it's a story made up by the King to keep forces abroad in check with scaremongering,' he said.

BY LEE M. COOPER

'I'm not so sure, do you really think they'd have an instructor tell us all that if there weren't at least some truths to it?' Max replied,

'I suppose we will see in time, Jarrel. Let's just focus on our studies for now and keep why we actually joined in the first place at the forefront of our minds.'

'On that we can agree pal, I mean who wouldn't believe the world will be a safer place with us protecting it, right?' Jarrel chuckled to himself.

'Let's just pass first mate, there are many years ahead yet and this is not going to be an easy ride by any stretch,' said Max.

Later that day during a free period, Max found himself sitting in the temple library. There were a fair amount of student's in there, as he sat alone on a simple looking wooden bench in a corner of the room, watching the world go by around him. As he began to daydream, it still came somewhat of a shock to him, that he'd finally started on his path into a new world. One he'd only previously dreamed about as a child.

He'd found and pulled out a book from one of the shelves marked, 'Ancient Magic & The World before us.' As Max looked around him to check nobody was looking, he hovered his right hand over the cover and tingled his fingers with a smile. He closed his eyes and concentrated……then, the pages began to flip open slowly. He could feel the gentle breeze upon his face of the pages brushing by, as he suddenly opened his eyes and slammed his finger onto the first random page the book stopped on. Max's smile started to turn into a more serious look, he

Might & Magic

focused his eyes onto the details that lay before him. There was a paragraph in the particular chapter that spoke of the royal line of Kavlos. Of how it had first begun with King Kavlos himself, who incidentally, the great city was named after.

The pages told of how he founded the city centuries before as a traveller with his people. The city was naught more than a few ruins that could be used to shield his people from the harsh lands around. It also spoke of how King Kavlos was blessed with magical abilities, able to heal the wounded & the sick. He was looked upon as a saviour by his people and over the coming years, they would begin to construct what would eventually become the great city it was today.

Max's mind drifted off again as he imagined what he would've been like, and what he accomplished. He dreamed of what he himself, might one day accomplish. After all, he had always been a confident young man when it came to his abilities. Even his mother had always been very vocal and encouraging to push his powers from an early age.

Thwack!

'Ouch, what the hell. Who threw that?!' Max shouted, as a heavy book entitled 'The Power of Leadership,' smacked him in the back of the head. The culprits came from the next bench just behind him.

They appeared to be a pair of twins, an identical male & female to be precise.

'Looked like you could do with a reality check there, dreamer boy!' sniggered the young male.

BY LEE M. COOPER

'Forget it Ni-ar, he obviously ain't worth it. If he can't even sense and stop a dumb book hurtling towards him, how is he ever gonna stop a bullet or a fire ball!' said the young female twin next to him.

They both stood up and walked over to Max, who was sat rubbing his head and looking quite disgruntled. The two looked slightly older than Max, around their early twenties if he had to guess and so were probably already well into their second or third year of the academy by now. They both appeared to have long black hair tied back, the young man's into a bob and the young women's was into more of a pony tail style. They dressed similarly in the standard academy provided student robes, the man's was a dark brown colour whereas the women's was dark purple.

'I am Ni-ar,' said the man.

'And I am Ji-ar,' the young women jumped in.

'And as you can guess, we are twins. Not just in looks though, but in power to' said Ji-ar.

'My sister is right, and that is a crucial bit of information for you right there. You see, because if you ask around here.... We're kinda a big deal. We have been favoured by Master Kain of the KingsGuard himself as ideal candidates for the King's personal guard,' Ni-ar continued.

'Well isn't that just splendid for you both' said Max with a sarcastic tone.

'Heh......just letting you know, we heard about your family name. Starheart, wasn't it? Your father has quite the history around here it seems. We will be watching you

Might & Magic

closely with great....shall we say interest,' Ji-ar said in an almost suspicious tone.

They both stepped away slowly giving Max a look of contempt, before turning to walk away.

BY LEE M. COOPER

Chapter 4: In the service of a King

Several years passed. Max had graduated with promising grades both academically and physically speaking and had now been serving in the King's empire for just over five years. He was now thirty years old, and his looks had dramatically changed. He now sported a shaved head; a

Might & Magic

full unkempt beard and his face bore its fair share of scars, each telling its own story.

His most recent orders having been assigned, were to escort and accompany Onix of the KingsGuard on a peacekeeping mission. Max had passed his initial exams many years prior, and Onix had always taken a particular liking to Max and had personally requested his presence there. He had been present sporadically at the beginning of his training, but as time went on and the years passed, more and more Onix would come to watch Max practising his magical abilities. He witnessed him grow into a confident and powerful young sorcerer, amongst his class.

Onix had befriended Max the first time they was banded together in battle, and often spoke of what an asset he was becoming. Though at this point, even though there was always a student and master like relationship between the two, there was also a mutual respect and sense of comradery between them.

'Sergeant Starheart, you seem troubled. What ails you, tell me?' said Onix.

'Is it that obvious, master?' replied Max as their shuttle jetted its way towards their destination high above the white, fluffy clouds. 'It's just......I've been serving now for a few years and well, I'm not so sure I'm getting out of it what I wanted when I first set on,' he said.

'Oh? And for what exactly was it you were hoping for? You have grown and harnessed your skills into a fine young sorcerer, perhaps one day you may even become a high mage and serve the King himself directly,' Onix remarked as if a proud father would to his son.

BY LEE M. COOPER

'You appear to be on a path many others dream to be on, is that not as you wanted?'

'Don't get me wrong, master. I am truly grateful to serve in the King's empire and I am pleased with how my skills have developed, it's just.... I was hoping to learn more about my father by now and why he disappeared when I was just a boy.'

'Ah, you never made mention of him to me before, but I am aware of your family's lineage in the King's service and of your father.'

'You do!?' Max sharply snapped, 'Master what do you know, please.... please tell me.'

'I recall him as a young sergeant, not unlike yourself. It did not take him very long to work his way up through the ranks. He made the rank of High mage within his first two years of service if memory serves me.'

Max stared at Onix with anticipation, as if hanging onto his every word.

'He became quite a prominent figure; his power was remarkable. I had not seen someone so gifted in at least a thousand years. That is what drew me to you Max, I had a feeling you may follow in your father's footsteps. Pay heed mind, today we have a job to do and must remain focused but upon our return to Kavlos, you should seek an audience with Thamir should I be able to arrange it.'

Onix then looked out of the window of their shuttle into the distance, then turned back to Max.

'He was on the last known mission that your father disappeared on .... perhaps he can give you the further information you seek,' he said.

Might & Magic

Max looked down with a slight frown of his brow, visibly disappointed that his line of information was cut short. From out the window, the clouds began to thin and waver as their shuttle began its descent, rocking amongst the rain and wind. The pilot turned and spoke up.

'Prepare for landing and brace for a bumpy descent, looks like we will be landing in the middle of a storm.'

Their destination was the city of Mazire, it was a fair distance from Kavlos but still the most neighbouring town thereafter. It lay southwest from there and was surrounded by lush forests. Though it was quite a flat city with many low buildings, a far cry from that of the grand royal city of Kavlos. It was nonetheless a thriving city and had been an ally of the empire for around five hundred years.

As the shuttle touched down in the city's eastern region, a man could be seen waiting by the landing pad, flanked by several guards.

'Looks like were expected master,' Max remarked as they slid their shuttle door across and disembarked to meet their welcoming party.

"Greetings my lords, my name is mayor Haradin and I offer my thanks for your visit. It is not every day we are visited by the great Onix of his majesty's KingsGuard,' the man spoke.

Upon observation as he stood just behind Onix, Max visually scanned him as a small man no older than his mid-fifties in age, dressed in very lavish looking robes, green & golden in colour and intricately decorated with various flamboyant tassels, ruching, and other high-quality materials. He surmised this must have been down to his

BY LEE M. COOPER

political status as the mayor of the city. He had a slight mistrusting look about him, a sneer that Max could see from a mile away. He knew master Onix was probably thinking the same, after all, he had been around long enough to be an expert in character assessment within a few seconds of meeting anybody.

'Not at all, the King always tries to make time for his allies, as often as he can spare it,' Onix replied.

'Please, this way' Haradin said with an extended arm, guiding the way towards an open door just behind where he was standing. As Max, Onix and the two other soldiers accompanying them followed behind the mayor, the conversation continued between them.

'In accordance with what we have already sent to the King prior explaining our dilemma, I thought it prudent to elaborate' Haradin said with a sneering smile.

"Please, proceed.' Said Onix.

'Although our cities have long been allies and friends since the uprisings of the old rebellions, we do unfortunately now fear that the ever-increasing disruptions among the townsfolk, seem to be more frequent. Unlike us, they do not think the empire's rule is neither just nor necessary. They see it more of an ever-present dictatorship and do not understand why they should answer to, with all due respect, a King who does not ever seem present, and an emperor that as far as they are concerned, doesn't even exist.'

Onix stopped in his tracks and stared at the mayor, who's smug smile slowly drooped to a worried, more frightened look.

Might & Magic

'I can understand these concerns some of your citizens may have Mayor Haradin, but rest assured the emperor's rule is a just one, for without our great empire to help keep the peace in check, I fear the world would be in a much darker age than it already is.'

'Oh, I agree certainly my lord, which is why I am sure that if you could just speak to the masses in our public hearing this afternoon it would go an incredibly long way to help change their minds, perhaps put them at ease as it where,' Haradin replied.

As the men continued, they came upon a long a glass corridor which connected the landing area to a more administrative building, suddenly the first real look amongst the city of Mazire was upon them. As they walked along, the branching streets below could be seen with visible shadows weaving in and out of the various streets almost like ants in the distance. This was indeed a populous city; Max had only ever heard of Mazire but was little aware of its actual size. Shuttles and airbuses zoomed by, in a multitude of different directions, high above. As with aircraft all over Omeria, they were all run by magically powered engines which were developed and produced, from Kavlos' imperial R&D division. This was a massive contributing factor to the wealth of Kavlos.

Through just a few more short winding interior corridors which were lined with all kinds of administrative and government dressed personnel, they arrived at a set of iron double doors.

Mayor Haradin remarked.

'Beyond these doors, lie's our grand town's square balcony. We use this for various declarations, announcements, and weekly public speaking events. Although like Kavlos, we are a fairly, albeit not as technologically advanced, modern city, we do by tradition keep public speaking very much at the forefront of our community. We feel that personable touch is what makes us different from others, ' he sniggered.

Onix stood with his arms folded and glanced at Max with a stoic look, as Max looked back in the same way.

'Then please, let us proceed and see if we can't put the people's minds at rest mayor,' he then said.

'But of course,' Haradin replied with a sneering grin once more as he slowly opened the doors.

A momentous pop of applause and cheering suddenly erupted from hundreds of the city's residents standing far below as the doors were tossed open. The balcony itself was no more than ten feet wide and only stood a few feet away from the interior doors. The main square below was itself an erected building which stood distinctly from the other nearby buildings, which were all connected by long skywalks. It was clear not all the population of the city could obviously be present at these hearings, but a select amount of important and wealthy citizens of the city were always invited. The mayor took a slight bow in front of the ruckus crowd as he then began to speak to them with a boom of joy in his voice.

'Citizens of Mazire, I bid you all warm greetings on this not so pleasant of days' he said, as he looked up at the grey sky from which rain was still moderately pouring down.

Might & Magic

'However today we are blessed by one of our King's very own personal guard and representatives, none other than the legendary sorcerer.... Onix everyone!'

There was a mix of cheers, boos and a smaller portion of the crowd which didn't quite know what to say and so stood silently in anticipation of his next words.

'People of Mazire,' Onix started, as he placed his fists on the balconies' stoned flat surface.

'I stand here before you today to hopefully answer any qualms or concerns you may have, regarding our empire. I am aware that not everybody understands the logic & will of the emperor and the royal house but be assured that I am here as a representative of those powers to answer your questions.'

Max, standing just a step behind and to the left of him, could not help but notice the clouds gathering ever darker above as he glanced up. Onix's armour glistened a bright green as the rain fell upon his shoulders, trickling down over the intricate designs that were embellished upon it.

There were shouts from the crowds.

'How do we know we can trust the emperor? How can we trust the King? How can we trust you?!'

'Long live the King!'

'Why does the emperor not show himself, what has he to hide!'

'Onix the great wouldn't lie!'

'We are a free people; we do not need to live in fear of the empire!'

The raised voices came from every direction before him. As he was about to speak again however, the thunder began to rumble more like a deep growl now. Vibrations

BY LEE M. COOPER

could be felt underfoot, almost like it was about to erupt from the very earth itself. Flashes suddenly lit up the sky as frightened gasps blurted out from the crowd. Max raised his arm and covered his face attempting to block the sharp, blinding light from his gaze.

'Master, something doesn't feel right' he said to Onix with a confused tone in his voice.

'Kain'. Onix muttered under his breath, 'What are you doing here....'

Then with a clap and a whaling bang, a gigantic bolt of brilliant blue lightning crept down from the darkest cloud above, hitting directly into the middle of the crowd below! Screams from every direction beckoned out, flames burst forth underfoot as waves of lightning bolts crackled throughout the ground. Gaping cracks opened all around and stone chunks from the raised square flew about in every direction, Max's first instinct as he waved his hands about seemingly manipulating forces around him, was to create a force field of energy around him and everyone else on the balcony. Debris and fire spat out at Max but were deflected off his force field, keeping them safe from harm.

'Is anyone hurt?!'

Max shouted to the crowd gathered around him. Many below lay dead and severely burnt in the square. Max's legs were Shakey, but he showed no sign of struggle holding his casted spell high aloft.

'No, I think we avoided the worst of the blast luckily, what the hell is going on!' panicked the mayor.

Might & Magic

Onix said 'I do not know, but I will find out soon enough. Max, I trust you can escort these people to safety.'

'Yes, but master where are you going?' Max said confused.

However, before Onix even had a chance to answer he had already vanished into thin air, leaving nothing but an aura of green mist where he stood seconds earlier. The people below that were left unscathed albeit apart from a few scratches and cuts, had mostly now dispersed in terror. Max couldn't help but think that this was more than a mere freak accident of weather, after all, it seemed very precisely contained to the balcony square and he had never seen lightning act in that way or magnitude anywhere in his life!

'Everybody back inside!' shouted Max. Once they were all inside to safety and had closed the balcony doors, Max placed his hands on the mayors' shoulders. He had grown pale like stone in his complexion, with cold beads of sweat that had already begun to trickle down his forehead.

'Mayor Haradin, I need you to try and stay calm. Me and my men here will find out what exactly happened here but I......no, Mazire needs you right now to help calm the townsfolk down, and initiate safety protocols. Can I trust you to do that please?' Max asked him.

'Ye, yes...yes......yes of course sergeant. Please do what you can, I fear ill forces are at work this day' he whimpered.

Max signalled the two masked soldiers that accompanied him to follow, as he ran back the way he came before, retracing the steps back along the now cracked glass corridor, outside now portrayed a much

BY LEE M. COOPER

different & darker picture than their earlier journey across. Lightning and torrents of heavy rain now battered the daytime sky, and flickers of fire could still be seen rising from the remnants of the town square.

As they reached the air pad once more, heading back towards the shuttle, Max called for the pilot, who was still aboard, to prepare for take-off. Suddenly Max stopped, held his arms out once more and conjured another shield of energy as he shouted.

'Everybody down!'

He was uncertain of exactly how he could sense it, but he could almost feel as though another projectile bolt was about to come crashing down upon them and in that very moment, another came hurtling down from the grim, now terrifying sky. It struck the shuttle with deadly accuracy and a mighty force, the soldiers who accompanied Max also shared the pilot's fate as they were out of reach of Max's powers.

The shuttle disintegrated under the force, leaving a plume of flame swirling into the sky. Again, Max managed to hold his nerve and protect himself, even under a might clearly closer and more impactful to him than before.

A few moments later as Max was still gathering himself on the floor, the dark clouds began to disperse at an unnatural pace, the rain stopped, and the blue sky could be seen once more as if it was a mere passing shower. Max lowered his spell. He now knew something sinister was afoot.

'There are only a select few with that kind of power over the elements' he thought to himself.

Might & Magic
'What the hell……'

BY LEE M. COOPER

Chapter 5: An Emperor of Legend

Approximately 3,500 years ago…. the great citadel of the emperor.

Onix, Thamir & Kain marched with haste into the emperor's citadel, having been summoned by the emperor himself. As they walked through its great wide halls, decorated with monuments erected to the emperor,

Might & Magic

they couldn't help but observe their surroundings. High stain glass windows stood tall from floor to ceiling, and great rays of radiant light beamed through each one. They portrayed important moments of the emperor's history and his various conquests throughout his last fifty-year reign.

They varied, from being portrayed as a young, great warrior slaying many in countless battles for his King & country, to him being knighted as a protector of the realm and establishing the first regiment of his own personal mercenary army. As they continued to walk throughout the halls, the stone statues depicting him began to appear greater in size and more exaggerated. Enormous murals now flowed on into another room, of the emperor clad in armour riding atop great beasts and dragons, slaying his enemies. Then, darker still became the depictions. Paintings high up told a story of how the emperor gained increasing power, too powerful to control, eventually usurping the King long ago.

It appeared to the uninitiated that the emperor wanted to keep a King and royal family around, though for what exact purpose was unclear. Perhaps, it was to keep the citizens of Kavlos from rebellion, perhaps something else. The KingsGuard however knew the truth, they had served him since the first remnants of his army gathered. Great sorcerers of power unseen up until that time and knew many secrets about him.

As the three men finally arrived at the enormous doors to the emperor's private throne room, two knights approached them clad in golden armour. They were at least seven feet in height and appeared to be utter brutes

BY LEE M. COOPER

of beings. They marched menacingly in unison, their great unsheathed swords of pure diamond, suddenly staked into the ground before them as they stared the three sorcerers' deep into their eyes. The knights' faces could not be seen. They were shadowed in darkness, under a heavily decorated helmet of gold and naught but a set of red glowing eyes could be seen about them. Clearly these creatures were not human, they proceeded with a blood curdling grunt.

'We are here as we have been summoned by the emperor himself, now please, stand aside creatures of shadow' Thamir exclaimed as all three seemed unphased by the two behemoths in front of them.

They growled once more before one said in an eerily low and creepy voice 'You may enteeeerrrrrrr, the emperoooorrrrrr is expecting youuuu'

The doors began to creak and crack as they slowly started to open. The knights stood back to their original positions either side of the doors but continued to stare ominously. Once the doors had fully opened the three KingsGuard slowly walked into the room as the doors slowly started to close again behind them. They now stood in the emperor's throne room, the most private and off-limits room in all of Omeria where only a very select few other than Thamir, Onix & Kain, were ever admitted an audience into.

The room was truly one of a kind. It was constructed with nothing, but the finest natural materials known on Omeria. Marble, gold, and diamonds of every kind littered the room. The walls were of the purest white marble and

Might & Magic

crystal, a beautifully intertwined mix seen nowhere else on the planet. It was clear the emperor enjoyed extravagant and exquisite tastes and visually enjoyed impressing upon his guests, his status as the ruling power in all of Omeria.

Though the KingsGuard had entered numerous times before, they were always still breath taken upon entering. As they began to approach the emperor's throne along the golden paved walkway directly in front of them, they finally laid their eyes upon the deity like presence of the emperor himself.

The emperor sat upon his crystal made throne as they closed in. He sat, slouched in his seat. His right arm resting on his armrest with his chin upon his fist, looking oddly bored yet expectant as though waiting for some news. Although the emperor had been the grand ruling power now for a great number of years, he had not aged a day since his inception as emperor. He did not appear a day over his mid-thirties still. Even the King of this era certainly appeared more aged, being around sixty and very grey at this time.

However, the emperor still looked youthful. He was an incredibly handsome man by appearance with long blonde flowing locks that seemed to gleam amongst the diamonds of his crystalline throne. He stood about six feet five inches tall at full height and had a medium length, dark blonde beard. Atop of his head rested a silver circlet of pure white gold with a brilliant purple amethyst diamond in the middle of his forehead. His attire was that of a knight of the realm, only naturally more imposing by design. It too was silver in colour but laced with diamonds. It did not exactly look battle ready but more decorative and flamboyant in its nature.

As Thamir, Onix and Kain reached the steps just before the throne, they each knelt to one knee.

'Your excellency, you summoned us?' said Onix.

'I did,' replied the emperor.

'For many a decade now, I have ruled as your emperor and undoubtedly without you three being my eyes and ears out in the world, I am sure our new empire would not have grown anywhere near as quickly. For that I thank you all enormously. However, I've need of you now for a different task. I am appointing you three as the official KingsGuard. From now on, I want you to be shown supporting the King in whatever his needs may require.'

'Of course, my emperor but doesn't his orders come directly from you, my lord?' Kain confusingly asked.

'Indeed, you are correct Kain, however, it has come to my attention, that there is unrest in Kavlos, amongst a number of other places, and we cannot afford to be seen to be overthrowing the royal house, which has stood for a thousand years. I will not lose the influence we have so justly gained. A mass rebellion of any kind is the last thing we need during the empire's infancy,' the emperor said with distain as he looked away.

'Very good my emperor,' replied Onix.

'Now, you may leave.'

As the emperor then causally waved them away, the three stood and turned to begin walking away.

'Kain...you wait here' the emperor then said in a commanding voice.

Might & Magic

As Thamir and Onix glanced at the emperor then back at each other in a slight bemused look, they continued walking and left the room. Kain remained as commanded and stood at the foot of the throne stairs. The emperor then sat back and began to raise himself up, he was now stood at full height and his presence became quite fearful. He shined like a living diamond in all his angelic armour as he slowly began to walk down the stairs towards Kain.

'Kain, ever since we first met all those years ago at the temple on my pilgrimage, back long ago when I felt as young as I still look now. I have trusted your ruthlessness more than the others. Your will to get things done, the others...I know how they really look at me, with distrust that I will abuse the power bestowed upon me. I know what I must do for the kingdom of Kavlos…. for Omeria!' he shouted.

'My emperor, I am and always have been certain that you are the one that legend speaks of. Although we remember not our creation, we do not forget our purpose on this planet. To serve and protect that which legend speaks of, he who will lead Omeria to everlasting peace for all eternity!' Kain said with a fierce confidence in his eyes.

'That is why we took you in, trained you in our ways once we could feel the already present power within you. I know my lord that you will become the most powerful practitioner of the mystic arts in existence, and then will our task on this world be complete.'

The emperor smiled as he leaned his head back, his eyes were a glow, and he placed his hands firmly on Kains shoulders.

BY LEE M. COOPER

'Ever my most trusted servant Kain, know that although we must give the King our support and in doing so show support to the people......should the King make, any.... shall we say grave error of judgment then you will be my 'swift sword of guidance. With the power to correct any misguided courses the King may place any of you on. Remember, trust in me your emperor, to make the right decisions for the good of Kavlos & Omeria.'

'Yes, my emperor of course but what of Onix & Thamir? They will be suspicious and may act out against me' said Kain.

'Thamir may be loyal to me as are you. Or he may betray me. I do not know his destiny. Onix however, I sense great conflict within him. He may interfere with my plans for Omeria, so I will keep them both close by my side. You must act swift & silently, should I deem it so.'

'As you wish my emperor' replied Kain with a bow.

Later that day, Thamir and Onix were outside the King's quarters at his castle, overlooking the setting red sun as it began its descent over the lofty mountains, opposite the kingdom of Kavlos.

'Thamir, what make you of the emperor's behaviour. Do you not find it strange that he confides in Kain too much without our knowledge?' Onix turned and asked.

'I do not know of what the purpose is of these secret meetings between them' he replied.

'But I do still believe that we must keep our trust placed firmly in emperor Malvik. You sensed the great power within him that day he came upon us at the temple, the same as I. We must believe that he IS the one we were

Might & Magic

destined to follow as foretold by a much higher power than us my brother.'

Thamir continued.

'I'm not so sure, at first I did believe he was the one and perhaps he is but the ever-growing power within him combined with his greed of late years has cause for my concern.'

Thamir stroked his chin as his eyes scattered about finally setting upon the crimson sky as the sun slowly began to disappear.

Onix decided to leave him to his thoughts and returned through the door behind him, into the King's quarters and following through directly into the King's throne room. The two had been in conversation with the King earlier in the day to inform him of their new duties to him, following on from the emperor's commands. The King was not present upon his throne as Onix entered, but instead was reading a book in the library over in the next room.

The King's throne room was not near as grand as that of the emperor's and was far older. It was simple, small with grey stoned walls all around, with a few large windows. A small number of flame-lit torches gave the room its light, as the darkness outside began to draw in. The throne itself was clearly the spectacle of the room, being made of pure white marble with golden leaves adorning it all over. It was truly a work of art from a more ancient time.

As Onix approached the King who sat at a small reading desk lit by candlelight, he halted and bowed.

'My King, I thought I would check in on you before I retire. Is there anything you need my lord?' He asked in a softly spoken voice.

BY LEE M. COOPER

'Onix, I am old. I feel old, I look older and every day I feel my grasp on my people loosening and the emperor's grasp tightening, like a snake around my throat.'

Onix glanced down at the floor and clasped his hands behind his back. He replied.

'My King, you must understand that the emperor is not here to overthrow you or your people. Please, allow me to indulge you in a story. Many moons ago, me and my brother's arrived in this world. I do not remember when exactly or how, but we were born of a bright light, that much I do remember.'

'Around us was a temple with mural's all around, that depicted the many great evils of this world in constant battle against the forces of good. However, one such picture that stood out, was of a being encased in light wielding a mighty, heavenly sword. This being we believed to be a man of destiny, who we have been sent here to find and protect at all costs. This man is believed to be the one who will end all conflict and evil in Omeria' he said with certainty.

'Onix, the emperor has been ruling here since I was a much younger man. The day you three and he arrived here with these...these...prophecies, with your magic. We trusted you with our city. Our lives also, but there is still so much I do not understand. This magic you display is like nothing I have ever seen before. To speak to the very earth as you do is godlike and far superior to the only magic, we previously knew of! And I still do not understand where you came from. You said when you arrived in Kavlos, that there would be no interference with

Might & Magic

the monarchy and that the emperor was simply here to help guide and protect us all. I barely get an audience with him anymore. More and more, I get the feeling that my rule and the democracy of the people are being ousted.'

At this point, the King slammed his book shut, stood up and walked to a nearby window looking out into the distance.

'I feel powerless, Malvik is not the same man who came here all those years ago to help us. I sense a great evil about that man. And Kain......I do not trust him; evermore do I find his grim stare upon me, as though he is plotting something sinister. I do not know what to do anymore Onix, I have never felt more unsure of how to lead my people' the King said with an almost defeated tone. He turned to look at Onix.

'You are the only one I trust of the emperors' servants, the only one who has kept counsel with me and the only one I feel honesty with.'

'My King, you honour me with your kind words, but please rest now. We have much work abroad to do in the coming days and you will need your strength, if you are to accompany us on your next assignment.'

'Yes, I suppose you are right,' said the King. 'I shall retire shortly. Thank you Onix that will be all for today, I think.'

BY LEE M. COOPER

Chapter 6: Reckoning

Present day.

Kain pushed open the grand doors as he left from the emperor's citadel in Kavlos, his walk had a certain cockiness about it, and he sported a smug grin as though he was pleased with himself about something.

Might & Magic

The day over Kavlos was calm, the sky was blue with just a few small clouds. Otherwise a beautiful day, with just the gentlest of breezes. As Kain continued to walk down the private mountain pass that linked the emperor's citadel to the royal palace, he couldn't help but feel the breeze begin to slightly pick up. Kain thought nothing of this and continued on his way. As he furthered his way down the pass, he came between two huge mountain walls as the pass bent and curved around between them. Kain stopped as his good mood began to turn sour, and a look of confusion befell his face. He sensed a slight rumble beneath his feet which slowly grew into a vibration strong enough to shake him off balance falling to one knee.

'What in the...' Kain began to say before he was abruptly cut off, and forced into the cliff wall by a powerful, invisible force of air. As he tried to stand to his feet, he could feel himself being held down to the ground by something.

'I should've known it's you Onix, release me damn it!' he shouted as a human silhouette emerged behind him, out of a green mist in the air.

'WHY KAIN, WHY DID YOU DO IT!?' Onix shouted, as he was now fully present behind him, continuing to hold him down.

'Gah.... release me!' Kain shouted as his body began to emit bands of electricity all around him. His eyes turned a razor-sharp blue as they crackled with power and a thunderous rage, the sky began to rumble & turn darker......and then......... he unleashed a powerful wave of electricity from his body, knocking Onix back across into the other cliffside wall!

BY LEE M. COOPER

As Onix staggered himself back to his feet, they both gazed at each other from across the mountain path as if in a standoff.

'You know damn well what the King was trying to achieve in Mazire, to further strengthen our friendship with their people and then you.... YOU KILLED INNOCENT PEOPLE THERE!' Onix erupted with a rage in his eyes.

'And you remember what our first orders were Onix, right? From the emperor...to correct any misguidance in the King's commands as we see fit!' Kain shouted back at him.

Onix disengaged his fighting like stance and composed himself, closed his eyes and took a deep breath.

'And what exactly was misguided about that, Kain? About making a truce, making allies, to settle any qualms some of the people there may have had about the empire hmm, tell me? The people were unsure enough before, but they are not stupid Kain. They will know that was no mere freak act of weather, rather that foul play was at work!'

'The emperor and his empire need no naysayers in his vision for peace, they are a distrustful people. They did not want to help the emperor, they wanted to probe for information so they could attack him!'

Onix looked down with a glare of disappointment as he rubbed his eyes with his hand in frustration.

'Kain, you must see.... Malvik......these are not the decisions of a sane man, let alone a man said to bring about global peace? If it were not for his paranoia and warmongering, there would already be peace!'

Might & Magic

'ENOUGH ONIX! I will hear no more of your heresy, the emperor has always been right about you. You cannot be trusted!'

At that moment, a swirl of intense flame danced between the two from out of nowhere, eventually settling in the form of Thamir.

'That's enough, the both of you!' said Thamir. 'We are meant to be working together, that is our purpose. Onix, whether you deem it appropriate or not, if the emperor has given orders which Kain sees fit to act on then we must discuss this with him. Kain, having said that, what were you thinking? You acted alone and without our council!'

'I do not have to discuss anything with you two, I have informed the emperor of my actions. And if you must know, I was acting under his direct command. He doesn't trust Mazire but cannot exactly be seen to be acting against the King upon his every command. That would only incite riots in the city' Kain replied.

'Thamir surely you must see, the emperor has grown paranoid over the years. The more power he has gained, the more afraid he is of losing it. The shield of power for example that covers this city. No one has attacked in a thousand years. Is it even necessary? It just makes the people uneasy' Onix said, pleading to Thamir's better judgment.

'Listen, this is neither the time nor the place for this conversation' Thamir stated abruptly. 'Kain, go and see to the city's patrols. Onix, as for you the King wishes to hear your report on your visit to Mazire. As dire as that may be, you must report to him….and do NOT tell him of the emperors' involvement.'

And with that, the three teleported away in their own respective way's. Kain raised his hand and with a crackle of electricity from the heavens, his whole body was enveloped in a bright blue energy before he vanished into the sky, with a thunderous clap.

Onix shook his head in disappointment, then slowly withered away into a green mist which blew away with a gust of wind.

As for Thamir, he paused a moment to think about the words that had been exchanged. He had been in a personal conflict of sorts for quite some time but hadn't made it known to anyone else.

On one hand he could see Kains stance, that their born purpose was to support the one legend spoke of. However, on the other hand he also saw Onix's point of view and questioned himself whether emperor Malvik was indeed this individual.

For now, he decided to pause these thoughts. He knew he needed to seek out answers. Where these answers would come from however was a different issue. Maybe, he thought. Maybe he would need to go back to the beginning…back to the Temple of Creation. What if the legend was misinterpreted? What if all along, they had followed the wrong person? Thamir stroked his chin as he deeply pondered this thought. Then just as he appeared out of a burst of flame from nowhere, he just as swiftly disappeared with one.

Might & Magic

Back at the Imperial academy, a place where Max had now lived out a vast chunk of his adult life, he had seen many changes over his time there. For one he now lived in the upper suites of the academy where all soldiers resided once they had progressed their training and graduated. As Max's door to his apartment unlocked & swung open, he stood in the doorway visibly exhausted. He closed the door and staggered over to his kitchen counter and poured himself a glass of water. He still could not understand what he had just witnessed in Mazire as he stumbled to his sofa and sat down. The view from here was beautiful over the city. A full-length pane of glass functioned as the viewpoint across the city from his apartment. He looked out at the bright cloudless sky contemplating what had just taken place, trying to make some sort of sense of it all.

Knock, knock, knock!

Max snapped out of his trance as a knock came at his door. He put his glass down, stood up and walked to the door to open it.

'Jarrel, what are you doing here?' Max asked his old friend stood in the doorway.

'News travels fast around here mate, I heard you were stranded in Mazire and had to call in for a transport. You ok, what happened?'

'You better come in bud' Max stood aside as Jarrel walked in and leaned by the window.

Just like his friend, Jarrel too had graduated around the same time as Max and had seen his fair share of warfare by this point. Though his appearance had not altered too much in the last five to ten years, he was not the cocky

BY LEE M. COOPER

young man he used to be. He also on occasion, had trouble containing his powers. He had been involved in a particularly nasty accident in a nearby village several years prior. Whilst trying to blow out a hole to save a number of trapped villagers in an avalanche, he inadvertently created a blast too large and vast. Instead of helping the situation, he had regrettably made things worse and killed many innocent people that day in the process. He was never quite the same after that day.

'Honestly man, it was like nothing you've ever seen' Max started as he filled him in on the details of his recent trip. By the end of his retelling of what had happened, Jarrel was sat on the sofa with a puzzled but somewhat worried look on his face.

'Max, I don't like it. It's the KingsGuard, it reeks of them I know it.'

'I have to admit, I've had my suspicions as well' confirmed Max.

'I don't know why but I'm certain they are involved mate' said Jarrel, as he continued.

'Let's take the last five years for example, how many times have you heard of strange goings on, on missions? Or resistant outside parties suddenly falling in line after one of them has visited. Or politicians going missing mysteriously. I was on a reconnaissance mission just the other day and whenever I mentioned the KingsGuard they seemed to cower in fear and shouted demon, demon!'

Max made a worried look to his friend. 'Jarrel, I don't think its master Onix. I've come to know him quite well over time and I know his loyalty to the King is absolute. He

Might & Magic

is a good man. Thamir I'm unsure of, sometimes he seems dedicated and then other times very distant & mysterious. He makes me feel…. uneasy at times.

Master Onix seems to think he may know something about my father before his disappearance, so I need to find and talk to him for that matter. Whereas master Kain……he's always been different to the other two hasn't he'

Jarrel nodded agreeingly 'Yes, that was my thought too. I've heard he's less supportive of the royal family than the others and that he has regular dealings in secret with the emperor himself….so I've heard anyway. And he's never in a good mood.'

'Listen, I'll be out of the academy for a couple of days from tomorrow on leave. Figured I would see some family, catch up ya 'know. Why don't you see if you can find master Thamir and ask him whatever questions you may have about your dad. He may even confide in you about what happened in Mazire, see if he knows anything?' Jarrel said.

With that Max smiled at him and nodded. Jarrel then stood up and walked towards the door.

'I'll see myself out, just make sure you get some rest tonight and think about what you want to ask. Time with any of the KingsGuard is rare as you know so make it count!'

Jarrel then placed his hand on Max's shoulder as if to reassure him, as he smiled, walked out, and closed the door behind him.

Meanwhile, approx. twenty miles southeast of Kavlos in the barren desert of Nelwei, an unpopulated drought like

BY LEE M. COOPER

region, Thamir whisped into existence from his pure fire & flame like form. Around him other than a vast burning desert of which the sun beat down on relentlessly, wasn't much more other than a few, sand-coloured rock formations. However, Thamir knew this area all too well, as he followed the rock formations down through twists and turns, he shortly came into a gaping valley. This valley was known as the valley of creation and placed at the very end into a hollow recess of the surrounding valley, lay the Temple of Creation. It was here that Thamir, Onix and Kain first awoken a millennia ago. From where and sent by whom, was a question that had evaded them all their lives.

As Thamir approached the old temple, he had forgotten how plain and unimpressive it looked from the outside to the average person. This area was not exactly a place that was visited often. In fact, Thamir recalled the day Malvik happened upon it by chance, he and his brothers were so surprised anyone found it at all. Thamir held out his hand as a snake of fire wrapped around his arm and blasted at the temples unassuming wall creating a portal of otherworldly glyphs.

He stepped through it as the portal closed behind him. There he stood inside the temple, in its true form. A gigantic room surrounded by beams of light that shone down from the ceiling, at various points throughout. Ancient depictions littered all around the walls and directly in front of him, lay the three thrones were he and his brothers spent so many years waiting. Waiting for the one to appear before them. Thamir stared at the thrones as his memories began to come rushing back to him…

Might & Magic

3,650 years ago……

Within the Temple of Creation, three powerful mages sat on three thrones of pure energy.

These mages were Onix the grand mage of the earth, who could speak to Omeria itself. He could feel when the planet was in pain and likewise when it bloomed with energy. This was the source of his power.

Thamir the second mage was the scion of fire and creation. His powers grew as Omeria's population did. It was said that he could gift life to areas otherwise devoid of it.

And finally, there was Kain the third mage. The mage of weather and destruction. Legend foretold that he had the power to destroy any wrongdoers of the planet and to control the weather of the planet to enable Omeria to thrive for the best.

These three mages were created to work in unison, to protect the planet and oversee her growth. This was of course, until 'The one' would appear. It was deciphered when the three first came into existence within the murals and depictions in the temple that one day, that someone would appear with the strength to bring about a continued peace. Until that day came, the three would patiently wait. One day however, one day as the three sat waiting as they always did, a portal opened before their very eyes.

The mages leaned forward and stood in astonishment…. after thousands of years, could it be that the one has finally arrived?

BY LEE M. COOPER

A slender, bandaged & bloodied hand suddenly became visible through the portal at first. Followed by a head of long golden hair and then the full form finally appeared of a young man. He looked like a weary traveller of sorts, tired with multiple cuts and bruises about him, early to mid-thirties and although he did not look the most impressive of men, he had a certain strength about him.

As the portal closed behind him, he looked stunned at the three of them for a moment.

'Wh......where......where am I? What happened? A moment ago, I was in a dune like valley......leaning against an old decrepit monument of sorts. I put my hand out to lean against it when light began to appear before my very eyes! And now......I'm here! Tell me, who are you? Are you friend or foe?' asked the young man.

'That depends on the manner of your arrival. Do you have a name?' Onix asked.

As the young man suspiciously glanced at them unsure of what had happened or who these beings were, he chanced that introducing himself may hopefully lead to some answers. Attacking was by no means an option, he was weak, weary from days of travel and he seemed obviously no match for the three mysterious figures before him. Malvik was young and many things, but a fool was not one of them.

'Malvik, my name is Malvik. I have been travelling on a pilgrimage of sorts for three days. My steed is no longer of this world, exhaustion, and the harsh sun and scarce food here has almost finished me as well. Now please, tell me.... where am I and who are you?'

Might & Magic

Thamir replied 'No doubt you have many questions, and we shall do our best to answer them. My name is Thamir, and these are my brothers Onix & Kain. We have been waiting here a long time, for one who prophecy tells us will save Omeria from self-destruction, once and for all.'

Malvik stared at the three for a moment, his eyes jumping between the three before bursting out into a deep laughter.

'Ha ha haaaaa, ah ha…. sorry….y….you are serious? And you…you think this 'one' might be me? I am just a weary traveller; do I look like a saviour?' Malvik asked.

Kain then spoke 'no one has ever happened upon this place accidently, as it is not a place to accidently happen upon. You must be one born of an immense inner power otherwise the portal would not bring you here to us. We are what you might call 'sorcerers' of power the likes you will have never witnessed.'

Onix continued 'it is foretold in our destiny, to impart the knowledge we have unto The One. This must be you,' he said as he waved his hand across to his right upon where the mural began on the temple wall.

As Malvik looked across to the wall then back at the three, he decided to entertain the theories all the same and walked over to where Onix pointed to.

'As you can see' Onix began to explain, 'the ancient pictures painted here depict all sorts of evils running rampage on Omeria eventually putting the world to flame and ruin. An evil so powerful that even we cannot save Omeria from it……Until a warrior of light appears.'

Malvik's eyes followed the paintings as Onix explained them to him until he mentioned a warrior of light at which

BY LEE M. COOPER

point his eyes widened and then squinted back as he moved in for a closer look.

'My……God. That warrior…. he looks just like me' he muttered in astonishment.

'Now you see, now you see our reaction is warranted by your arrival. Please, we understand this must be a lot to take in. Allow us to reinvigorate you, we have food, water, and all manner of supplies you may require. I believe your pilgrimage brought you here to us for this very reason. Will you please accept our offer at least?' said Thamir.

Malvik looked at the three one by one still in an amazed manner and then back at the mural.

'I accept' he then replied.

Over the next coming days, weeks, months and even years Malvik became their student and spent his time learning the mages mysterious ways. Their teachings of magic and how to bring out Malviks inner talents for sorcery that he never knew were there. They trained him meticulously in swordsmanship, battle tactics, alchemy, history, survival tactics and anything they believed he may need to succeed if indeed he was the prophesised one set to bring about an everlasting peace.

Several years had now passed and the three mages had discussed among themselves, and agreed the time was finally right for Malvik to leave the temple and begin his new campaign for peace. It was agreed that the best place to start, would be the royal palace in the kingdom of Kavlos.

'Today Malvik, is a grand day. Today you begin your life's purpose. We will leave this temple and with it your past.

Might & Magic

We march for Kavlos, there we will appeal our aid to their King. They will be unsure at first, as we are foreigners to them, and they will not understand our power as their ways are primitive. However, we must convince the King to hear us' the three mages explained to Malvik.

'I am ready my masters, you have trained me in ways I never thought possible, enabled me to use magic of which I never knew existed. By my honour I swear, I will do all in my power to fulfil my purpose.'

And with that statement, Malvik and the three mages set of on the beginning of their journey to bring about an everlasting peace to Omeria.

Present day.

Thamir stood within the walls of the great temple, looking repeatedly at the various murals trying to piece together what he might have missed along with his brothers.

'I just don't understand, I have never studied something so hard and for so many years and yet I'm convinced I'm missing something, somewhere...' Thamir grumbled to himself.

He sat against the wall to pause and try to clear his mind. He took a deep breath and punched the wall in frustration.

kchuk...tick....tick...tick......clunk!

The noise came from the brick he had just punched, as though a mechanism had kicked into gear. Thamir jumped to his feet and looked back at the wall. Before his very

BY LEE M. COOPER

eyes he witnessed the last few panels of the mural begin to flip over and spit out eon's worth of dust.

'Oh my god' Thamir dropped to his knees and what he saw...he couldn't believe. The panel that previously depicted a hero of light saving the world, had now flipped over to create an image of a demonic shape wreathed in shadow and fire seemingly enslaving the people of the world!

'....... what have we done' Thamir broodingly said to himself.

Might & Magic

Chapter 7: Force of Nature

At the southern border of Kavlos, lay the city gates. This was the only point of entry into the city due to the energy shield that enveloped Kavlos from top to bottom. The gates were usually pretty well guarded and the security there ran a pretty tight operation at all times, after all

BY LEE M. COOPER

nobody would want to explain an unauthorised security breach to either the King or the emperor.

On this particular day however, there were six heavily armoured soldiers patrolling the gates, usually there would be a minimum of twelve however several had been re-routed to a disturbance in the marketplace.

'Another exciting day stood watching the gate…. wish we could've gone to sort that market fight out. At least it would've given us some action for once' said captain Matheus.

'Hey, at least you don't have to spoil that pretty face of yours bro' replied soldier Willis jokingly.

'That is true Willis, it's a shame my modelling career never took off, I suppose it's a perk of your job though getting to work with a handsome devil' Matheus winked back at him.

The road directly ahead of them that led into Kavlos was long, narrow, and very direct. The only view the security at the gate would usually see is the mountainous regions that surrounded their kingdom, some grassy plains with limited wildlife inhabiting it and some tall trees scattered throughout. Other than that, it was fairly uninspiring with the actual city itself being the crown jewel of the area.

'Man do you ever get tired of…. wait…. you see that?' Willis stopped in his sentence as something caught his attention from out of the corner of his eye.

'What?' his patrol partner asked curiously. Willis waved to summon the other patrol guards from the security booth.

Might & Magic

'What, is there a problem?' they asked as they emerged and then paused in their steps as they all looked ahead into the distance with somewhat confused and wide-eyed faces.

From what could be seen and heading directly towards them from the mountains on the horizon, were huge dust clouds and what looked to be a convoy of sorts.

'The bi-noc's!' Willis shouted to Matheus as he reached for them instantly without delay and passed them over. Willis scrambled to get a precise view lock on whatever was headed towards them. The others looked on in eager anticipation.

'I see......several armoured vehicles. Looks like tanks, hovercraft carriers....and.... EVERYONE DOWN!!!' he suddenly screamed out!

Four, five soon it was eight missiles that hit the energy field around Kavlos. The force field was designed to dampen any impact or explosion made to it but the sheer volume and power with which the missiles repeatedly hit, couldn't stop the force of the explosions that ensued.

The entrance to the city was completely engulfed in flames within seconds, though the shield still managed to protect Kavlos, the impact was inadvertently diverted towards the security gate. For the guards this was unfortunate to say the least.

The six guards currently on security detail were immediately launched into the air with the force of a tornado and were dead before hitting the ground. This in turn, set off the city's security alarms and defence protocols.

BY LEE M. COOPER

All level five and above military personnel to report to the southern gate immediately, this is NOT a drill! REPEAT. All level five and above military personnel to report to the southern gate immediately, this is NOT a drill

The distress call beckoned as loud as a bell over the tannoy at the academy and sirens rung out aloud. Max, who was pacing around his apartment jumped to attention immediately upon hearing it and grabbed his battle armour from a nearby cupboard, running out of his room with haste as his heart raced.

He made his way to the hangar bay, running now with great pace towards the nearest transport he could find preparing for take-off. He could see on the monitors above security footage showing the southern gate in flaming tatters, and an unknown military or mercenary force of sorts screeching through to a halt as their transports began to unload dozens of armed soldiers.

'Pilot, get us up and to the gate now!' He shouted as he boarded the transport shuttle which already carried three other soldiers. As it lifted and accelerated at top speed out of the hanger doors and into the air over the northern sector of the city, it joined dozens of others all racing towards the distress call location at the southern gates. Upon approach which only took a minute or so Max could see troops below firing back at the foreign invaders. Whoever these were, they appeared to be well armed and prepared. They had two tanks positioned either side of the entrance, Max turned to the others on board.

'Whoever these are, they have two Mythos Z-1000 tanks aimed right at the security barrier, they've breached the

Might & Magic

main gate but looks like they are trying to torch down the plasma shield generators with those things. Once they get through them, they will be into the main city, we CANNOT let that happen. Pilot take us in, you three follow my lead. They may be well armed and dangerous but ill dare say they've never experienced the full fury of the King's best!'

The pilot lowered the shuttle to around twenty feet from the ground as requested by Max. He then slid open the side hatch and jumped into the air. Descending he held his left hand in front of him and produced a blast of powerful green magic which had a dual purpose. Firstly, it slowed his descent and enabled him to land safely, also its force projected several of the invaders back into the tanks knocking them out instantly. Max followed this up by holding out his right hand and created a long katana shaped sword made of pure magic. Its blade hummed and crackled with the green glow that had become synonymous with Kavlos magic. The other troops arrived shortly afterwards behind Max, though descending in a less impressive manner by rope.

As Max continued cleaving his way through the unknown and disguised enemies in front of him, he could not help but wonder in the back of his mind who these intruders were or why they were here. He demonstrated unbelievable elegance & precision with his katana, using his left hand to emit a shield protecting him from incoming fire whilst cutting, swinging, and cleaving through his enemies with his blade. He was able to make each swing explode with a green flame to help maximise his damage.

Once more imperial soldiers began to arrive as backup the imperials began to easily gain the upper hand. Their

BY LEE M. COOPER

combined training was too overwhelming for the invading force to push back, and Max alone had killed at least fifteen or so by now, eventually turning his attention to one of the tanks. It was starting to become somewhat of an irritance to him.

Dodging two shots aimed at him from its turret, he launched himself into the sky and somersaulted onto the roof of one of the Z-1000's. Using his energy blade, he cut through its turret with ease like a knife through hot butter and then used his magic grip to grab a hold of the upper half on the tank. Sparks and wires could now be seen bursting from the tank. He closed his eyes and concentrated. Then as creaks, cracks and the sound of breaking steel could be heard, mixed with screams from its pilot, he managed to rip the roof off from the tank completely!

Several imperials had to stop for a moment to witness this impressive feat of power & sorcery. Max then tossed it aside with ease revealing a terrified tank pilot screaming, this was quickly silenced as Max relieved him of his head with a swift slice of his katana.

Now the imperials were beginning to push back the invading stragglers back out to the open plains around the city. The only issue now was that the remaining tank had turned its attention to Max, it locked its aim onto his back and fired its remaining payload. Four consecutive shells which materialised from the tank's turret as flaming energy balls. Max heard it fire, he turned but in a moments breath he feared this was it. He was too pre-

Might & Magic

occupied elsewhere on the battlefield to notice the shot coming from behind him.

He closed his eyes as he prepared to embrace the inevitable.

'This is it' he thought to himself.

For a moment he felt at peace, he knew one day he would likely fall in battle defending the kingdom he had loved and fought to protect all his life. He could accept that if he was going to die, then at least it was on the battlefield, a warrior's death. A split second felt like an eternity as he was waiting but…. nothing happened. He opened his eyes to see the shells amazingly floating in mid-air along with the tank!

Max was speechless and not even a thought came into his mind as he looked on in shock. A young women held them aloft in a force field of her own before launching them with an almighty push right back over the great plains from whence they came. As the smoke cleared there were no survivors left of the invading party. Debris and bodies were strewn about everywhere however, there were only minimal casualties on the part of the royal guard.

Max walked across to the young women who had saved his life just moments ago, he slowed his pace down as her face now came clear into view. Suddenly he recognised who she was.

'Moranna, long time no see.'

'That's lieutenant high mage Moranna to you sergeant Starheart,' she quickly corrected him.

'Apologies, it appears I owe you a debt of gratitude for back there. Thank you.' Max smiled nervously back at her.

BY LEE M. COOPER

He remembered Moranna from back in his old academy days. She was gifted from an early age like him, though she always had difficulty fitting in socially and making friends. She very much preferred to keep her own company and was usually very distrusting of others. However, where this originated from was any one's guess.

She was of a slim yet toned build and only slightly smaller than Max in height. She was naturally beautiful, had deep brown eyes with long wavy flame red hair that flowed freely down her back. Moranna always seemed profoundly serious, she was always very career oriented and was the type who knew exactly where she wanted to be from an early age.

Her uniform was that of a typical female lieutenant of the imperial army, the standard graphite shaded body armour decorated with imperial crests and elegant designs. The arms were covered in a lightweight yet extremely durable mesh like material that travelled down reaching her gauntlet covered forearms. The gauntlets themselves had numerous functions including a comms device if required, a concealed multi survival tool and a tracking chip that could be used for pursuit missions. She had a short dark blue cape that flowed from her shoulders down to just above her knees which bore the imperial insignia. Her legs where encased in a continuation of the mesh like material found on her arms but combined with armour plating that covered over her thighs, shins and finally finishing at her leather boots. It was fair to say she was indeed a striking presence to behold.

Might & Magic

'You're quite welcome soldier, although it seemed you didn't need all that much help. That was quite impressive. I haven't seen you in action like that before, but I can see why master Onix speaks so highly of you now' Moranna said with a smile.

'You have any idea who they were or where they came from?' Max asked inquisitively.

'I have my suspicions, me and my men have only recently returned just last night to debrief the King from the western territories, after we had lead's that some conspirators of the King may have been camped over there.'

'And did you find anything?'

'When we arrived, we scoured the whole area where we had been tipped off. We found an underground camp of sorts in a cave, lots of anti-empire propaganda and some empty crates of ammunition was discovered there but there wasn't a soul to be seen anywhere. However, we did find tracks, looked like single file tracks and ones that would match the Mythos tanks we just busted up here. We followed the tracks left behind, but they vanished around forty miles due south of here. Looks like these were the one's though and if I had to guess, whoever these were I'll wager there will be more of them.'

Max squinted his face and his eyes darted around as if in a confused ponder. Just then a sudden gale picked up around them and with a whirl of leaves about them, appeared Onix in one of his usual trademark arrivals he had become so famously renowned for.

'Master Onix!' Moranna & Max both exclaimed as they bowed respectfully.

BY LEE M. COOPER

'What brings you to us?' Max asked as he lifted his head.

'I am glad to see you are both safe after that attack, I would hate to lose two good mages in one day especially former pupils of mine. That being said, the King wishes to see you both. He would like an update on the situation here as soon as possible.'

They both looked at each other nervously before looking back towards Onix.

'Of course, master. We will be there right away' Moranna said as she stood to attention.

'Very good Lieutenant, the King will be expecting you. Now if you will excuse me, I have other pressing matters to attend to.' He then turned and walked away to address some nearby soldiers.

Max and Moranna agreed to take the shuttle there that Max had arrived in earlier as the pilot was still awaiting his next orders. They both walked to its side door hatch, Max slid it across addressing the pilot.

'Pilot, take us to the King's palace post haste.'

'Roger that sir' he replied as he began flicking and pressing various switches overhead in the cockpit to prepare for take-off again.

'I'm glad you showed that scum just what the empire is capable of sir.'

The shuttle began to lift off back into the air as Moranna and Max took their seats and strapped in. By this time emergency fire crews had already swooped in to start tackling the fires left at the gate below and new patrols had already replaced the dead ones.

Might & Magic

The King's palace was a place that few rarely saw and even less had visited.

'Have you ever had an audience with King Gorak before?' asked Moranna.

'No, you?' Max nervously replied.

'Only a couple of times, the first was a few years back after master Thamir personally recommended me to head a surveillance mission overseas.'

'Wait, overseas.... you mean the one to the city of Bloom, the one where a battalion of terrorists were said to be stationed and holding up hostages? The same mission where the surveillance team led by some relative unknown female captain, not only found said terrorists but thwarted the whole operation there?' Max asked with building excitement.

'The very same' Moranna smugly confirmed with a smirk across her lips. 'I didn't realise the story was so famous' she laughed.

'The King was so impressed with my report that he promoted me there and then to the position I'm in now. Then the other time was just last night to debrief him on my latest findings. He seems to find utilising my reconnaissance skills to be the most effective use of my talents apparently.'

Max scratched his head in slight irritancy but still smiling.

'Well, I am happy that you are moving up through the ranks. I just don't understand why I never got those kinds of opportunities for progression in my career. I mean, master Onix and I have been on all kinds of missions together and we've had quite a lot of success in our time. Why did he never put me forward for promotion.'

BY LEE M. COOPER

'Max.... I'm sure you will. After seeing a taste of what I saw out there today I'm sure the King cannot help but notice. Maybe that's part of the reason he wants to see you now?'

Moranna turned to look at him, with a cautious yet concerned look.

'Listen there's something you should know about King Gorak...he's....'

She looked down unsure of the right words to use next.

'He's changed. I don't know what it is but between my first and last meetings of him, he seemed a very different man. I remember he was once very kind spirited, joyful even and very much a man of his people. When I saw him last night bearing in mind this was around four years since, he seemed low, exceptionally low and disheartened. I am even a little worried for him. After I mentioned last night about what we had found with the conspirators and all he just didn't seem to care. He said he would step up security patrols and not to leave the city for a few days, just in case of an attack. Well, you saw the lack of soldiers on the front gate today, I just don't know where his head is at. It's almost like he's given up on life.'

'Maybe it's since he lost his queen. Queen Miya was his rock after all, so it was said' Max suggested.

'Maybe so, listen all I'm saying is whatever expectations you may have or preconceived notions about him, well just expect the unexpected, ok?'

Max peered out of the shuttle window as he could see they had just come over the great northern wall and into official royal territory now. They then quickly passed back

Might & Magic

over the academy temple and proceeded to elevate north. This was now an area Max had never formally entered. The high-rise palace tower gleamed high up in the daylight, standing ever proud. Their shuttle then began its descent over the main castle walls. Before they could land however the pilot had to call in to security for landing permission.

'This is shuttle 0XC1-125 requesting clearance to land under direct orders from the King, I have Lieutenant high mage Moranna Vix and sergeant mage Max Starheart aboard, over.'

There was a brief momentary pause as there was nothing but silence over the comms air. Then a voice barked back aggressively.

'0XC1-125 you are cleared for landing in bay 18, arrival escorts will be on standby, over.'

As the pilot settled the shuttle into the allotted landing bay Max and Moranna slid the exit hatch back open and were greeted by six of the King's personal guard. They stepped out and were immediately sprang upon by one of the guards that stood before them.

'You two, follow me the King is anxious for your report' he commanded.

'As you wish, please lead on' Moranna responded.

The personal guard stationed within the palace were unlike anything Max had seen in the empire up to now. They were in plainly decorated silver and blue armour. Unlike the armour worn by most other ranks, the King's personal troops wore only the highest quality materials. Expense was clearly no issue, they branded dual swords one sheathed on their back and one sheathed by their

BY LEE M. COOPER

waist. Both looked more for decoration than actual use with gold and blue grips, blue ribbons draped down from the hilts and there were ornate designs on both blades. These swords were not to be underestimated, however, if a time came for their use, they were more than efficient enough to wield, lightweight and deadly in their proficiency.

Their faces were covered by matching silver & blue helmets which were topped by some type of long dark animal hair that ran down their backs. No outside features were able to be seen, behind a slim dark visor. The body armour was sleek in design but forged of only the toughest steel, a rare steel said to be mined from underneath Kavlos itself and nigh impregnable by neither blade nor bullet. Even by what Max had seen in all his years prior, they were quite an intimidating site to behold.

They marched towards a gigantic door at the base of the King's tower, along a path that was lined either side by more of the King's personal guard all stood with perfect width apart from one another, facing inwards. They arrived at the door and came to a halt as two sensor beams either side activated, and scanned the party from head to toe. An affirmative high pitch 'beeping' noise sounded as if to confirm permission, then cogs & chains began to turn inside, opening the heavy doors.

Once open, they proceeded through as they then slammed shut behind them ominously and was led down a brightly lit corridor decorated with antiques of every kind, both familiar and foreign in nature. Max could not help but notice the King was clearly a man of taste and a keen

Might & Magic

collector of various antiquities. Vases, paintings, ornaments, and weapons from all over the world were proudly on display behind thick panes of glass. They entered an elevator at the end of the grandly furnished corridor where two more guards stood watch like still statues.

'From here you will proceed alone, this leads directly into the King's throne room. Do not keep him waiting any longer' one of the escorting guards said.

Max and Moranna stepped inside the brightly lit circular room as the doors slid closed behind them and the elevator quickly began its ascent.

'He sure likes to make an impression on you doesn't he' as Max tried to nervously joke, but Moranna carried on staring straight ahead staying focused as she fumbled her fingers together.

Once the lift's mechanism came to a slow 'shzooomm' noise it stopped, and the doors slid back open again once more. Two more of the King's guards flanked the elevator doors as the two stepped outside and now into the main entry way of King Gorak's throne room. The two looked around at the apparent anciently decorated room, various alcoves opened either side of the room branching off into other areas such as a study, a library and a couple of rooms that were closed off from sight. Straight ahead lay the ancient King's throne unchanged from its original inception hundreds of years prior and still decorated with beautiful golden leaves on its pure white marble face.

King Gorak slumped and dishevelled looking sat atop it. The two mages dropped to one knee and bowed their heads.

BY LEE M. COOPER

'My King, we are here at your request to give our report on the attack earlier, should you wish to hear it now' Moranna said.

The King raised himself up from his throne, he was around fifty years of age with a slight hunch that made him appear smaller than he was. He wore his imperial royal robes which were richly adorned in blue & gold, in keeping with that of his personal guard. In his right hand he held the King's sword, it had a large golden hilt which led to a similarly designed cross guard and beyond that was a long wide blade fitted with gems either side that was so pristinely clean, it glimmered like a mirror. He took a step down from his throne.

'It is all part of Malvik's plan…. I know the truth…he is trying to end the royal line. He means to kill me!' he spat out in a panic stricken, raised voice.

Might & Magic

Chapter 8: A Lost Hope

Two days had passed since Thamir left the temple; he spent those days wandering the vast desert plains of Nelwei too ashamed to return to Kavlos just yet. After all what would he tell his brothers? That for hundreds of years they had followed the wrong person, that after all that time spent in the temple, they were tricked. And why

BY LEE M. COOPER

would they have been tricked? He wondered how he could have been so stupid, so blind.

The chances are they would not have believed him anyway. Onix possibly would've visited the temple to have looked but Kain, well Kain was far too invested in the emperor now to change his views & opinions anyway, he thought to himself.

The sun beat down hard on Thamir's back as he wondered with nothing but his thoughts. However, a benefit that gifted all the KingsGuard was the ability to withstand days without food or water and possessed much higher-than-average endurance to the elements. In Thamir's case, the fact he had gone days now without sustenance of any kind and had wandered the desert in thick heavy armour, came as nothing more than a slight irritance to him.

Thamir would walk a little and then pause, aimlessly drifting between the sand dunes lost amongst his own thoughts. As he stood looking out to the horizon on a particular momentary lapse however, he could hear a faint noise on the wind...it sounded like a low playful growl followed by a high pitch squeak. It was a sound he had not heard in many years but one that he knew belonged to only one animal. This was by no mistake the noise of a 'Sandbeak' and a particularly young one at that.

It was a welcome distraction to take his mind off things, even if only for a moment. He decided to climb towards the top of the raised sand bank before him to try and get a better view of where the noise was coming from. Sure enough, from the top he had a clear view all the way to

Might & Magic

the distant mountains that surrounded the forsaken dunes. What he also spotted much to his delight, was a rather large, furry wolf like creature. It was large enough for a human to ride. It resembled a horse in its stance but had razor sharp (albeit retracted) claws, a long stripey tail with a tuft of hair that protruded down the spine of it and a giant beak. They were natives to the sandy area and so this is where they got their namesake.

The creatures were known to generally be friendly enough although if they or their young felt threatened, they could be more than a handful even to the most courageous of warriors. Thamir however was no ordinary warrior.

He began to slowly approach the creature, making his way cautiously down the other side of the dune bank to try to disturb the creature as little as possible. The Sandbeak quickly acknowledged his presence just a few feet away and cautiously tilted its head inquisitively.

'Shhhh there, there my friend. Do not be afraid I mean you no harm,'

Thamir said as he slowly made his way towards it. He could not help but notice that this particular Sandbeak had been fitted with a saddle, harness, and reigns.

'Are you lost my friend, it appears you may have run away from your master, if I had to hazard a guess' said Thamir, as he gently held his hand out for the creature to sniff.

It made a cautious rumbling sound which eventually faded out into more of a purr once it could sense Thamir was no threat. Thamir was puzzled as to why this rather

BY LEE M. COOPER

friendly and domesticated Sandbeak was out all alone this far from any kind of civilisation.

'Let us see if we cannot find your owner, what do you say. May I?' he asked placing one hand on the saddle.

The creature gently knocked his hand with its beak as if it understood the question and was granting permission to ride upon it. So, with that Thamir gently climbed onto its back and held the reigns. He made a clicking sound as the Sandbeak lifted its head and began to sniff, as though catching a scent and began to follow it with a spritely sprint.

Thamir had always enjoyed the company of animals and other lifeforms on Omeria, and perhaps that's why the Sandbeak was so friendly towards him. In any case, the Sandbeak was able to cover much land in very short lengths of time, and within twenty minutes, it felt to Thamir as though seven or so miles had been covered. As they were sprinting along still amongst the barren dunes of Nelwei, the Sandbeak halted in its tracks and made a loud cheerful 'Squeeeek!' noise. Thamir wondered why it had suddenly come to a halt but then followed its line of site to a plume of smoke rising over the distant rocky cliffs.

'That where your master is? Well, what are you waiting for? Onwards my friend!' Thamir joyfully exclaimed as the Sandbeak seemed happy to run over in the direction of the smoke signals.

As they arrived at the horizon, Thamir could now see that over the edge was the shoreline and, on its beach, lay a small campfire where the smoke appeared to be coming from. As he made his way down, he could make out a

Might & Magic

figure sat beside the fire, stoking the wood burning upon it.

Thamir dismounted the Sandbeak as it squawked loudly as if with Joy and rushed over to the figure by the fire. The figure who was covered in a black hooded robe, was sat with a tall dark staff of sorts beside him. However, at the sound of the beast's joyful noises he immediately turned to look, stood up and beckoned out.

'Ohhh Indi! My beautiful girl I thought I had lost you forever to the sands!'

The man pulled his hood down as he petted the creature and was visibly very delighted by the site of it. He was an older man, with a long unkempt grey beard, bald with a slight crown of grey around the back and sides of his head. He seemed nothing more than a homeless old hermit Thamir thought.

'And I must thank you sir for bringing my beloved friend back to me, hmmm sir….?' The old man asked, waiting for his name to be returned.

'Thamir of Kavlos and…. you are most welcome. She is a splendid companion isn't she. I found her alone many miles from here in the middle of the desert.'

'She is indeed, and I would not wish to be parted with her again in a thousand lifetimes ha ha' the old man casually chuckled.

'Thamir, is it you say? Please come sit by the fire with me, the night is coming, and I must repay you with a hearty meal or at least the best meal that I am able to give presently ha ha'

BY LEE M. COOPER

'That is truly kind of you. It would be my pleasure, but I must warn that I may not be the best company at the moment' Thamir replied.

'Oh nonsense, any company is better than that of one's own, I am sure. Excuse me where are my manners, I have not even introduced myself yet. My name is Halgore and this Sandbeak is my best friend, Indi,' Halgore happily explained.

'We have been pitched up here for quite some time. Yesterday evening I was fishing as I usually do for our dinner, but I seemed to have disturbed something fairly large in the water. It was a great hulking shark of some descript, the likes that are not usually associated with these waters. Well as you can guess, Indi was startled and ran for the hill's ha ha. I managed to shoo away the monster but alas after searching a while for her, I had to return lest I too fell victim to the cruel sands. I had given up hope until just now, I fear I may never be able to repay you kind sir!'

Thamir thought the name 'Halgore' sounded somewhat familiar to him, but he couldn't put his finger on why. He smiled and replied.

'Please do not concern yourself with repayment, the reunion of two best friends is more than payment enough. However please tell me, as I am curious. You said you managed to fend off the sea monster, I do not mean to sound rude but.... you seem somewhat ill equipped to deter a monster of the oceans?'

'Oh ha ha. Well.... let us just say an old man has his ways...,' replied Halgore mysteriously.

Might & Magic

'Excuse me, I must tend to my friend here, she must be hungry and thirsty. I will make her bedding up for the night and then we can talk more over dinner. Now how does that sound young man?' Halgore asked Thamir.

Thamir smiled at the old man kindly.

'That sounds like the best offer I've had in a week!'

A few hours passed by as night now fell upon them, the sky was clear and blanketed by stars as the two men enjoyed their cooked fish by the crackling fire. Thamir had explained his situation to Halgore in the time that had passed. Halgore sat stroking his beard as he took in Thamir's story in slight bewilderment but also great interest.

'...Interesting.... most interesting. So, THE Thamir of the royal KingsGuard is eating MY cooking on the beach no less ha ha, these are indeed unusual times my friend,' Halgore laughed.

'And so for one of such unusual long life, you feel somewhat betrayed by someone or something, for this error in judgment I take it?'

'You could say that. I feel like I cannot go back to Kavlos just yet, at least not until I can calm my mind and work out what I will say to the others. I know my absence will not have gone unnoticed and so time grows short. Now you have heard my tale friend, but I cannot help but wonder more about yours. Halgore.... Hmmmm, why does that sound so familiar......' Thamir rubbed his chin whilst scouring his memory where he had heard his name before.'

'That's it! I am certain I've heard of a 'Grand Warlock Halgore' in the King's library. An old book that mentioned

BY LEE M. COOPER

Halgore in the same breath as emperor Malvik. Surely you cannot be the same?' queried Thamir with an almost stunned expression on his face.

'Ha ha. Indeed, there is no fooling you Thamir of the KingsGuard. 'Grand Warlock' is a title I have not heard in a long time, but I am the very same yes. In days long since passed before even your arrival to Kavlos, back when your emperor Malvik was still but an ordinary man.'

'Please, tell me your tale Halgore' Thamir impressed, anxiously awaiting his next words.

'I was once an advisor to Malvik. We lived in the same village, but I descended from an ancient line of magic practitioners. You call them mages now. Well, where I came from, they called me a 'Grand Warlock.' The men of the village believed Malvik to be their next chosen leader but first, in keeping with the village traditions, he must travel on a pilgrimage of the world before he could return and be deemed wise enough to assume his new position. I was chosen as his right hand you might say, the people believed my abilities to be a good omen and suitable enough to protect Malvik on his journey. However, along the journey we came upon the barren deserts of Nelwei, and we lost many of our party to the desert's brutality and lack of supplies. It became evident that we had taken a wrong turn in the maze-like sands and became hopelessly lost. One night whilst at rest, we were set upon by several sand crawlers. Disgusting, drooling, enormous worm like creatures. I used my magic as best I could to fend them off and we lost the rest of the surviving party members but when the dust had settled...Malvik was nowhere to be

Might & Magic

found! I feared he had been either killed or escaped but I could not find him anywhere. I searched for many years, even searching nearby towns and cities but alas my search was in vain. I had lost the one person who I had been charged to protect.'

Thamir stared in bewilderment.

'I do not understand though, that must have been centuries ago. Why are you still in these wastelands? And did you not hear when he had been appointed emperor of Kavlos, so many years ago?' he asked.

'Good questions indeed and I shall try my best to answer them. I'm assuming it's similar to you and your kin, but I too have been gifted with the secret to long life. Which is why, although somewhat aged, you still see me sat before you today. I must point out however, I have long life, but am not immortal!'

'The reason I still linger here, is from shame. Once I returned to my village I was shunned for my failure and banished to never return there. I suppose living here is a constant reminder to myself to be better. Almost like a chain I can never cast off.'

'Now as for your final question, yes. Yes, I of course soon heard of Malvik's coronation to his position as emperor, shortly after it was made. Though I purposely stayed away from Kavlos, I surmised that he no longer would have a need for me now that he had three ancient mages with him! And I felt shame towards him at first. As though I had failed him. It soon became apparent however, that he had become a greater power than we could have ever hoped he would be. Over time however I have heard whispers

BY LEE M. COOPER

and rumours that he may not be the emperor the people thought he would be.'

Thamir stood excitedly and peered towards the crashing waves of the ocean, the full pale moon above the horizon. Then he answered.

'Those rumours are true. Yes, I played my part in seeing him on that throne. And yes, it was our magic and a destiny we thought we were following justly, to imbue him with powers far beyond that of any ordinary being. Halgore, I fear that the power and long life he has acquired has driven him mad and paranoid over the years. We thought he was the chosen one of prophecy. Alas, I now see over the years how wrong we were.' Thamir said in a defeated tone.

'Hmm. It is quite something where you three came from or why you came to be at all. Even in my lineage of magical practitioners, there was never any mention of three mages as powerful as you. Or anything of a legend foretelling an ever-lasting peace for that matter. I sense a sinister plot is at work here, from powers beyond that even you and your brothers may not understand.' Halgore pondered a little more, stroking his chin whilst grabbing his long staff beside him.

'Listen, tomorrow we leave for Kavlos. We must convince the King and your brothers that the emperor is not this chosen one of prophecy, as you so call it.'

'But you have not left these deserts in years!? Are you sure you want to do this?' exclaimed Thamir in shock.

'Yes. It is decided. I think you are who I've been waiting for all these years. Maybe it is time for me to forgive

Might & Magic

myself at last and make up for my past discrepancies. Now let us rest for the remainder of the night, tomorrow will be the start of a new age. One where we will set things right my friend!'

BY LEE M. COOPER

Chapter 9: Knightfall

It was a Saturday morning, and Jarrel Jone's along with a select number of other imperial messengers had been sent out into the city of Kavlos to spread word and gather

Might & Magic

participants, for the upcoming annual tournament of Kavlos.

The tournament, also known as 'Knightfall,' was a yearly tournament held by the King and royal guard. It was funded by the empire and was used as an opportunity to discover new candidates that may serve in the King's personal guard. It was also an opportunity for mercenary's and warriors, to demonstrate their combat skills in the hopes of fame & riches.

Jarrel's appointed post this particular day, was in the market square. He was accompanied by two infantry soldiers and sat at a desk outside, displaying multiple posters aiming to gather attention.

'People of Kavlos! Step right up if you think you have what it takes to join the elite empire, this opportunity only comes around once a year and even the King himself will be in attendance! He bellowed out to the masses.

'Entry is free, and equipment can be provided on a first come, first served basis.'

There was always an excitement in the air every summer when the tournament came around. In the past, many of Kavlos' most famous warriors had been discovered here. Examples included Gunith 'The mighty,' Eldric 'The valiant,' Galen 'The Iron blade' and Havast 'The Indomitable.' Of course, there were also those who weren't so lucky, that fell in the tournament. It was very much a 'high risk, high reward' type of event.

From a few gathered civilians that cheered and looked on with anticipation, one man stepped forward from amongst them.

BY LEE M. COOPER

'Ah, fellow citizen please state your name and occupation' Jarrel asked with a smile.

'My true name is unimportant, but upon my travels……I've have been known as Shadowstorm,' said the man.

He was dressed in worn looking armour from an apparent distant land. It was unfamiliar to anything Jarrel had seen and quite different from imperial garb. It was rusted, a kind of rust colour mixed in with blemishes of light blue. Jarrel looked on with a gaze of slight amazement, he wondered if the man had purchased his gear from an antiques store at first.

'You seem, distracted my lord. Is there a problem?' asked the man.

'…no…no of course not ahem……Shadowstorm, was it? Replied Jarrel.

'And what is your age & occupation sir?'

'………knight of Omeria, forty-five.'

'Oh, that's quite an advanced age sir for this kind of tournament, are you sure about this'? Jarrel asked.

At this point, the man known as 'Shadowstorm,' stared at Jarrel looking insulted, and placed his hand on his sword sheath, as if ready to attack at a moment's notice.

'HOW DARE YOU SIR!' Shadowstorm shouted.

'Age has no bearing to a great warrior such as I! I have slain countless foes; numerous statues have been erected in my honour! Have you never heard of……. Shadowstorm 'The Just'! he exclaimed, turning to the crowds, and opening his arms wide gesturing his importance.

Might & Magic

There were grumblings of confused chatter amongst the crowd, in an attempt to calm the warrior down and defuse the situation, Jarrel had to think quickly on his feet.

'My apologies sir Shadowstorm 'The Just.' Only we people here of Kavlos are not the most well-travelled of folk. I am sure you are as deadly as you claim, you honour us with your participation.' He spoke.

'Hmph. Well.... that seems a more logical explanation for your apparent lack of education,' Shadowstorm muttered as he took a more relaxed and calmer stance.

'Tell me, when does this tournament begin exactly?'

'In three days, at the grand coliseum. We would ask for you not to leave the city until then please,' replied Jarrel.

'Then I shall educate you in three days young one, in the ways of true combat' Shadowstorm said, then turning away and pushing back through the crowd.

Jarrel said to his soldiers 'wow, it really does take all sorts in this world huh. Him I've got to watch!'

Back at the south gate, the security awaited the arrival of what they could only describe as two men riding on a giant wolf, bird like creature.

'Halt, state your names and purpose for your visit' asked the security officer, as two guards stepped forward to greet the visitors.

'Do you not recognise one of the KingsGuard anymore? Said one man in a full body robe, as he took down his hood.

'Master Thamir! My, my apologies my lord. I did not recognise you,' said the slightly panicked man.

'Do not worry. I understand my appearance at present seems somewhat...unusual, shall we say. And do not

BY LEE M. COOPER

worry, my steed here does not bite. I come with a guest from faraway lands to visit the King.'

'I see my lord. Then please proceed. We must advise caution however, this gate came under attack a few days ago. No one was seriously hurt luckily, thanks to lieutenant mage Moranna Vix and sergeant Max Starheart. We do not know the attacker's identity yet, but the King has asked us to increase the security detail on the city, especially with the upcoming tournament around the corner.'

Thamir looked over his shoulder to Halgore and then back to the security officer.

'Hmm, I see. Most curious. The city has not seen an attack in years. I would speak with Moranna & Max, but first I must see the King on a matter of upmost importance.'

'As you wish my lord' said the security officer as he stood aside and signalled for the gate to be dropped, allowing permittance to the two.

Meanwhile, at a local bar in the cities industrial sector, Max and Moranna had met to discuss the meeting with the King a few days prior.

'Moranna, I had no idea. He is not like any King I have ever known of. When you said he had changed, I didn't realise he was a nervous wreck of a man!' said Max alarmingly, as he supped his beer.

'Yep. As I said, he seems to now think that there's some kind of conspiracy theory about wiping out the royal line. I mean, although he didn't let much on for his reasoning why, I can kinda understand why he may think that. Let's

Might & Magic

look at the facts. He's the latest King in a long line of his ancestors that have been oppressed by the emperor in some way, shape or form. His beloved queen was found dead mysteriously in the palace, with no reasoning for her death. And he feels the KingsGuard are watching his every move!' Moranna explained.

'We need to find master Thamir, I haven't seen him in days. Master Onix seems to think he may know something about my father. Also, I think we should ask him about his thoughts regarding the King. I mean, he is one of the KingsGuard after all and he may be privy to his behaviour. I can't help but feel that him, the emperor and my father's disappearance are all linked together somehow.'

At that moment, a loud disruption occurred at the other end of the bar.

'Sir, I'm sorry. As I've said, I think you've had one beer too many' the barkeeper advised.

'Do you not kno...know...hic...who I am youuuuu scallywag! I'm hic, Shadowstorm the hic..... 'the just!' said the inebriated gentleman at the bar, slouched on a stool.

Max and Moranna looked across to see what the source of the disturbance was.

'Sigh, I'll go handle this. Listen don't speak a word of this to anyone yet, we will reconvene at a later time, ok?' Max said.

'No worries, let me know if you hear from Thamir and.... good luck with that guy! Moranna said with a smirk, as she got up and left the bar.

Max walked over to Shadowstorm, sat on his stool.

BY LEE M. COOPER

'Excuse me sir, I think as the barkeep has said, you've had quite enough already' as Max tried to reason with him.

'Listen here laddie, do you not hic, realise who you speak with? I am Shadowstorm hic, the just!'

'Well that as may be friend, but right now you just seem to me like Shadowstorm 'the drunk.' Now as a sergeant of the imperial military, I'm going to have to ask you to leave.'

'LEAVE? Leave...hic! Oh whatever. I'll leave alright......but you haven't seen the last of hic, me. I hope we meet at the tournament hic, then I'll show you, you imperial scoundrel.... hic.'

With that, Shadowstorm stumbled off his stool and clambered his way along the wall towards the exit. Before he exited, he straightened himself up, stood upright and then proceeded through the doorway. A loud clanging and a scream was heard from outside.

Max shook his head then turned towards the barkeep.

'That rust bucket drunk is entering the tournament? Jeez, I guess it really does take all sorts in this world huh.'

Over in the northern area of the city, Thamir and Halgore approached the King's palace. The kings personal guard had already allowed permittance to the two, the KingsGuard never needed any further permission than their already high status. As they came to the sensor protected gate that lay directly before the elevator into the King's throne room, a fairly grouchy guard stood in front of them.

Might & Magic

'Master Thamir, your absence has been duly noted by the King. What is your reasoning for this, and who is this you bring with you?' he asked.

Halgore spoke in his place.

'Are all of the King's soldiers this rude? You are indeed either very brave or very foolish to question a high mage such as Thamir, wouldn't you agree?'

'I, erm. Listen, I am only enforcing the King's rules. He has decreed that he isn't to be interrupted, unless by his own admission. Including the KingsGuard at present,' the rude, grouchy guard stated.

'He will see me, I am sure. I have brought with me a guest who he may want to speak with. On that, you may trust me. Now move' Thamir said, with a fire that lit up in his eyes.

The guard was taken back, and after flinching for a moment, he entered a code onto the control panel for the gate behind him.

'We will alert the King of your presence master Thamir, you may proceed.'

Cogs & Chains began to move as the doors began to part. Thamir stared the guard directly into his eyes, as he & Halgore walked through the opened gate and into the hallway at the end. As they continued through the inner hall of antiquities, they walked into the inner elevator tube, as it closed behind them and began to move.

Once the doors slid back open, the two walked into the throne room of the King, where he was sat hunched over on his throne and clutching at his sword. His crown looked crooked and dirty. Appearing pale, visibly sweating as droplets ran down his forehead, King Gorak gently rocked.

BY LEE M. COOPER

His eyes looked red and tired. It was evident he had not slept in days and upon approach, the King stared at Thamir with suspicion.

'Thamir. Where have you been? Why have you not reported in days? And who is this vagabond you bring before me, is he an assassin? Have you brought him here to kill me!?,' the King cried out in an accusing tone.

'My King please, calm yourself! This man I bring here before you, his name is Halgore. The reason I have not been able to report back in days, is because I have been on somewhat... of a personal mission.'

The King squinted his eyes wondering whether or not to hear them out. His mind was rife with paranoia and so any kind of audience at all was a blessing at this point.

'……Speak with haste Thamir but be warned, I am no fool. If this is some kind of trick to gain my trust or distract me in some manner, then it will not work' the King advised them.

'I assure you my King, it is not. Allow me to explain. I left some time ago as I had a great suspicion that aroused in my mind. The way Kain has been acting of late and the fact that the emperor is growing increasingly more dangerous and nonchalant. So I went back to the beginning sire, to the Temple of our Creation. And what I discovered there shocked me to my core.'

'Go on….' The King said unblinking and leaning forward on the edge of his seat.

'I believe that when me and my kin first brought emperor Malvik here, to Kavlos so long ago. It was under a prophecy that he was to bring peace, unity, and an everlasting light to the world. However I unearthed an alternate prophecy. Unbeknownst to us all, the prophecy in legend seems to also tell of one who would bring chaos and destruction about.' Thamir said, looking down with a troubled frown.'

The King didn't move but his eyes wavered slowly to the side after a moment's pause, as if in disbelief but also as though he was piecing something together in his mind.

'Yes……yes of course! It all makes sense now. Why my beloved Miya died. Why Malvik is watching everything I do!'

The King stood and began pacing backwards and forwards, rubbing his clammy hands together.

Thamir and Halgore looked at each other, a concerned glance occurred between the two.

Halgore then spoke.

'Oh mighty King Gorak, please, be seated. There is more to tell'

The King froze and glanced at Halgore, then quickly hopped back onto his throne, he hadn't seemed this interested in anything in quite some time.

'Halgore, was it? Please, continue' he said waving him on anxiously.

Halgore cleared his throat. 'It was at this point I happened upon Thamir wondering the deserts of Nelwei. I explained to him that, ages ago, I was a part of Malvik's company. I was his advisor and Grand Warlock at the time, or so I was known back then. To cut a long story short, we were separated in an attack one night and I never saw him again. I thought him dead until I heard that he became emperor of Kavlos. I hid in shame for many years and was completely unaware of this prophecy that Thamir speaks of. Now that I have learned it may have been a prophecy that was misread and could potentially lead to catastrophic events, I cannot help but feel somewhat responsible for him. As though I have a duty to see him dethroned from his position as Emperor of Kavlos.'

The King sat back into his throne and rubbed his forehead.

'I see. That is a lot of information to take in, Grand Warlock. If what you have told me is true, then you will have gained my trust. For the first time in a long time, I suddenly feel clarity in my mind, as though I am not going crazy after all. I need time to process all of this, who else knows about any of this?'

'Only us three in this room my King,' replied Thamir as the two looked on awaiting guidance from the King.

'You two will remain here in the tower, I shall have my men provide you with suitable sleeping quarters. I will think on this, and we shall reconvene tomorrow. That is all gentlemen'

Thamir and Halgore bowed, as they then exited through a side door in the room.

Meanwhile, at the emperor's citadel, Emperor Malvik was in conference with Kain.

The emperor was surveying his city out on his balcony, as yet another summer's day was drawing to a close. Kain lingered by Malvik's throne, gazing out at the last few rays of light, as Malvik spoke to him.

'The time draws near Kain, I can feel it. With the recent attack on Kavlos, it has surely stoked the King's paranoia

Might & Magic

tenfold. Soon, with a few more orchestrated invasions, he will snap! I am sure of it. And when he does, it will give me the perfect opportunity to show the people that their King is unwell & unfit to rule. Ha ha ha, yes.... this is perfect,' Malvik sneered with a sadistic grin on his face.

His bright, perfect white teeth gleamed; his long flowing golden locks of hair danced in the summer breeze. To the majority of Kavlos they thought him a sincere, benevolent emperor. One who preferred his position as a hidden hero, protecting his city as best he could, whilst leaving the King to continue his reign of the people. But looks can be deceiving.

Kain knew Malvik's darkest secrets, however. He was the only one Malvik confided in privately.

'And then my lord, who better to swoop in and selflessly put himself forward as grand ruler, Kain smugly continued to plot.

'Precisely. That way there will be no resistance and our army by then will be more than powerful enough to begin our campaign of domination! I will rule once and for all with an unfaltering clarity, one that this world has sorely needed!'

Malvik turned and stepped inside, wandering across his great throne room to a nearby bookcase. He looked for a moment, pushed a book inward on the centre shelf and waited as it flipped around and shot backwards, revealing a hidden button. Malvik pressed it before mechanisms began whirling, soon the entire bookcase started to slide to one side.

'A secret room, my lord?' Kain asked inquisitively with a surprised look.

'Come Kain, in here is the key to my future. The prophecy I always knew I had to fulfil one day...'

The two walked through the now open passageway, which lead down some stairs in a poorly lit tunnel. At the end, lay a wooden, plain looking door. Malvik brought into view an old key and unlocked the door. Inside, was a small round room with a glass case in the centre. A great barrier of green light protected the case, which dissipated as soon as Malvik clicked his fingers.

An ancient looking book was left revealed.

'My lord, what pray tell, is this?' said Kain.

Malvik replied.

'This Kain, is what I found buried beneath the Temple of Creation, one day. My destiny, waiting for the right time to use it....

The Book of Rebirth!'

Might & Magic

Chapter 10: Revelation

It was now the day before the Knightfall tournament, and it had been on Max's mind for some time that he wanted to speak with Master Thamir. Word had now reached him that Thamir had been back in the city and out of conference with the King.

'A perfect time to grab some time with him,' he thought to himself. The KingsGuard usually spent what little

BY LEE M. COOPER

downtime they had either meandering around the city or in their personal quarters in the imperial academy. He thought as he was in the same building, he would try reaching him first in the upper levels. From Max's apartment, it was just a short walk across the middle level walkway to the nearest mech lift. From this point, the whole of the academy could be reached from the ground entry level, all the way up to the senior level on the uppermost floors.

Anything above level 8, usually required a senior clearance card to gain access, though luckily, Max's rank permitted him access to those floors. So Max jumped into the lift and from his current position on level 5, he worked out Master Thamir's personal quarters would be located on level 12, the top level. He scanned his card and pushed the corresponding button, a light-hearted 'Ping' sounded as the doors began to close. In the cities mech lifts, it was never more than a few seconds to get anywhere and like everything else, it was powered by magic. Within a few seconds, the doors pinged again and swung open. He was in an area of the temple that he had only visited a handful of times in his whole lifetime. The decor of this topmost level was very grand and fitting of the KingsGuard, and few other senior officials that resided here. There was a long, deep purple carpet that rolled straight ahead from the lift and branched off like tree branches to different rooms. The floor underneath was made with white marble and gold torches lit the hallway on either side. A few paintings littered each side, mainly imperial in nature. As Max continued, he saw Thamir's quarters were clearly marked

Might & Magic

on the far most left of the rooms, as he stepped up to the grandly decorated double doors and knocked.

After a moment, almost to Max's surprise, Master Thamir opened the door and greeted him warmly.

'Sargeant Starheart, what a pleasant surprise. What brings you here?' he asked.

'Apologies master, I wouldn't intrude unnecessarily but....' he paused.

'You have something weighing on your mind, that much I can see is obvious. Please, come in' said Thamir, as he stepped back, opened his door fully and greeted him in with a wave.'

Max walked into the room, which he noticed was decorated with various dragon ornaments, paintings of Kavlos and many otherwise comfortable furnishings. It was simple yet elegant in its own way.

'I have just brewed a fresh pot of tea, please make yourself comfortable and I shall bring you a cup,' Thamir said.

Max made himself comfortable on a nearby plush looking leather sofa. This apartment naturally had some of the best views of the city and obviously the best of the entire temple.

'I sense something troubling you, let us stall no more.' Thamir said as he passed Max a cup of tea.

'Thank you master, ill cut right to it. On a recent mission with Master Onix, he mentioned briefly about my father. He said he was a powerful sorcerer, and that you accompanied him on the last mission he was on before he vanished all those years ago. I have to know, what happened master? What can you tell me of him?'

BY LEE M. COOPER

Thamir squeezed his lips together and sighed. With a slight nod, he proceeded to explain his story.

'You look so much like him, your father. I knew this day would likely come sooner or later. Well, it was about twenty or so years ago now, your father was indeed a powerful and wise sorcerer in the empire. I had worked with him many times before and on this occasion, we were tasked with leading a sizeable force overseas, to the eastern continent. Even the King himself was present, in the days when he was still very much active. Our mission was to secure a makeshift reactor. We had intelligence and evidence that alluded to forces abroad, who had created an unstable reactor, using stolen plans from the reactors of our own in Kavlos. The difference being that we have spent thousands of years perfecting our craft in renewable, clean magic. The reactor we found however, was crudely made from scraps and only understanding a fraction of the plans they had stolen. It was guarded by a small force of fighters, but we dealt with them swiftly. The bigger problem was trying to shut down the reactor before it became too unstable and caused a devastating explosion to the nearby town.'

'During the crossfire however, a stray bullet from one of the mercenaries hit a critical fuel pipe. Your father was the first to jump in and use his powers to try and contain the leak, as he knew it could blow at any second. I tried to run over and help him, but I was too late. The force was too great and the whole place exploded.... I managed to contain most of the ensuing carnage but....'

Might & Magic

Max placed his cup down on the table with some considerable force at this point.

'But what?' Max asked.

Thamir looked back at him visibly disheartened.

'Well……after I managed to use my power to absorb as much of the blast as I could, I surveyed the damage of the area in the aftermath. I was fortunate enough to be able to stop the blast from reaching the nearby towns & villages, but only a few of us survived. Myself, the King and a couple of wounded soldiers…. Max, I searched for your father but there was nothing to be found of him, no body, no items left behind……. nothing!'

Max sunk back into the seat.

'……I see' he said, staring at the cup on the table in front of him.

'Under the kingdom's laws, we could not pronounce him dead, as no body was ever retrieved. He was classified as MIA and the case was closed. I am truly sorry Max, for you and your mother. I should have told you sooner but, I did not have the heart to tell you. I see that was now incredibly selfish of me, and you had every right to know the truth. I just did not want it to affect the reason you joined the empire in the first place, or your future here,' said Thamir.

'On the contrary master. In fact tomorrow, I'm putting myself forward for the Knightfall tournament.' Max replied with a look of determination.

'What? Why? Isn't that for mercenaries to gloat about their fighting skills and attempt to achieve glory? Or for people that are not already enrolled in the empire? Why would you want to enter, Max?'

BY LEE M. COOPER

'Because it's my opportunity, to show the people and the King that I am ready to take the next step in my career. I know I am ready for more master. I don't know why master Onix never saw it in me, but I know I'm better than a mere sergeant. I want to make my father proud...wherever he's watching me from now.'

'I see. Well you had better get your name entered fast, if you're sure you want to do this? I have confidence in your abilities Max, do not get me wrong. However as I am sure I needn't remind you, it is also a very dangerous place, the coliseum.'

'I know master, I've made up my mind. This is my time now.'

Thamir nodded gently in acknowledgment, 'as you wish.'

In the southwest of the city, is where the great coliseum lay. It truly was a marvel of both technological and magical advancement. At the break of dawn the next day, Max had already arrived early to put his name forward to the tournament officials. Just as he had finished putting pen to paper, he took a step back to look up and admire his surroundings. Intricate constructional designs overhead interlocked with various steel and stone structures all around. The coliseum was oval in shape, and so there were many archways that branched off from the ground floor, to enable spectators to reach the upper tier seating areas. At full capacity, it could hold close to 100,000 spectators! It was another spectacular design of the kingdom and was truly world renowned. There would be weekly held tournaments both televised and for live

Might & Magic

audiences in attendance. However only once a year, was the famed 'Knightfall' tournament held.

It tended to be more brutal, with more variety of participants from both far and wide. Not to mention that in this competition, the rules were.....quite lax to say the least. There was a strange smell about the arena, which could only be described as a mix of fresh hanging flowers, singed flesh with just a hint of blood in the air.

'Well if I hadn't seen you here with my own eyes, I wouldn't have believed it!'

A familiar voice echoed, as Max turned to be greeted by none other than Moranna Vix.

'You really must be crazy to enter this, soldier. Though I do worry.'

'Hey, that's sergeant mage, lieutenant' he smiled, 'and no need to worry about me. I can handle myself.'

'I didn't say I was worried about you Max.' Moranna leaned over his shoulder and whispered in his ear.

'Listen, I know why you're doing this. What you think you have to prove. I get it. But just......watch yourself out there, ok?'

She gave him a gentle kiss on his cheek, as he blushed a little.

'I'll be watching you Starheart, good luck.' Moranna walked away leaving Max to consider what his tactics would be.

'Sir, sorry to interrupt but if you are ready you may want to inspect the armoury before the preliminary round's begin,' said a short and bulky arena guard, as he approached Max.

BY LEE M. COOPER

'Oh, thank-you. That won't be necessary' Max said, turning to look at the crowds began to enter into main coliseum seating ahead.'

'I have all I need, already.'

Might & Magic

Chapter 11: Round One

In attendance was everyone of any importance in Kavlos. As the thousands of public spectators in attendance began filling up the standard seats, in the upper tiers resided the politicians' booths, the wealthy aristocrats of the city and special VIP areas for anyone invited from out of the city.

BY LEE M. COOPER

Whilst the very highest area was exclusively reserved for the royal house. This included Onix, Thamir & Kain of the KingsGuard, King Gorak himself, his personal guard and even a grand throne next to the King for emperor Malvik. Though the emperor never showed in any year's past, and it looked like this year would be no different. Moranna took her seat in a senior imperial box, just to one side of the arena. She was joined by other lieutenant mage ranked officials, admirals of the imperial fleet and also a few sergeants who had privilege passes.

The idea of each battle round was that two randomly selected participants, would enter with a choice of their own weapon. Magic was permitted but nothing above a level three spell, as it was known. This basically meant nothing above a minor explosion was allowed, though there was a protective force field around the audience to keep them safe from any harm during battles. This usually gave any sorcerers or magic casters the advantage over the average mercenary, who only fought with hand-to-hand weapons. The main arena floor was made up of a raised steel bridge walkway. Two competitors would enter from opposing sides and duel it out, until there was only one winner left alive. On either side of the walkway, was an open drop which also randomly selected different booby traps such as spikes, flames, open pits or man-eating beasts. This made things a little more interesting and helped to even out any advantages certain individuals may have.

Might & Magic

'Welcome ladies and gentlemen, to the biggest tournament on Omeria. THIS....ISSSSSSSSSSSSSS......KNIGHTFALL!!!!'

An excited announcer pronounced, as he signalled the opening of the tournament. Confetti and balloons filled the open arena, as the crowds erupted with a roar of cheers. Bright banners were waved, in support of their favourite fighters both new & old.

'WALK THE BRIDGE! WALK THE BRIDGE!' Chants were heard, in anticipation of the fighters due for round one.

'We salute our illustrious King Gorak and his KingsGuard. We dedicate these games in your honour. FOR KAVLOS!' shouted the announcer across the speakers, as King Gorak stood and waved to the people below his royal box. Onix and Thamir stood in their full battle armour, side by side next to the King. Kain sat just in front of them, each of them placed a hand on their chest in salute to the crowds as they screamed even more. They were looked on almost as celebrities by the general public.

'Now, without further ado, are you ready for round one, people of Omeria?!'

The cheering continued, with occasional chants of 'BRING IT ON! BRING IT ON'!

'Then, introducing your round one contestant's. Contender number one, he has travelled all the way from Unthil on the western continent, he is known & feared as The Blade Butcher.........HE.....IS.......RAGMAR!,' the announcer shouted.

At that moment the door on the far left of the battle bridge opened, smoke gushed out first followed by a big, hulking silhouette of a man. The crowds applauded as the man made his entrance. He was a giant man, around seven feet tall, with a long dark brown beard with shades of grey in it. He was bald with tattoos on his head, which looked tribal like in nature. He wore a type of body armour not seen on the central continent before. It was a gunmetal grey colour, laced with miniature beams all over it, assumably this was meant to act as an extra layer of protection against blades, though it could easily be detrimental to the wearer if inexperienced. Ragmar did not look like a rookie however, he was around fifty years of age and looked as tough as they came. His choice of weapons comprised of a mace with spiked lasers protruding from it and a beasty looking sword, stained with blood that he liked to affectionately call, the 'Blood Breaker.'

As he made his way across the bridge to the centre, he didn't even crack one smile to the crowd. It was clear he was here for business and his nickname of 'The Blade Butcher,' look well earned.

'Annnnd contender number two, he hails from the neighbouring city of Mazire. He is a previous league champion of the coliseum here. HIS NAME IS.......BRAGORE!!!'

The door on the other side now slid open, again the theatrical smoke protruded out from the doorway followed by the latest league champion Bragore. He wasn't as big or brooding as Ragmar but was younger at around age forty. He was a battle hardened, experienced former bounty hunter. His garb looked almost espionage like, but was built for speed & agility, and he was well

Might & Magic

known for concealing fan favourite weapons in various places about his outfit. He walked to the centre and waved to the crowds.

'BRAGORE, BRAGORE, BRAGORE!' the crowds chanted. He was the clear fan favourite in this round it seemed. Neither were magic users, and so this would be a round of pure brute force and a little bit of luck!

They both faced the King, who was sitting high above and bowed, as King Gorak raised a hand in acknowledgement.

'Begin!' shouted the King.

Ragmar shouted as he lifted his blood thirsty blade over his back to slam down before him, immediately going in for the first strike and wasting little time. The bridge, though narrow, gave Bragore just enough room to duck and roll out of the way. Whilst squatting down to one knee, he used a concealed short blade that was retracted in his sleeve, to cut across the exposed area at the back of Ragmar's left leg. He let out a somewhat annoyed yell, before swinging down his mace in his other hand, knocking Bragore back but unable to pierce his hi-tech armour. Ragmar then turned and went to bring about his gigantic sword down again but this time with nowhere to roll, Bragore had to do his best to block and hope he had enough tricks up his sleeve to do so. He quickly hit a button on his left gauntlet, which flipped open a small panel, which he then swiped across with his finger as fast as he could. A small body sized shield then emitted, just in the Knick of time to block or at least keep Ragmar's sword at bay for a second.

BY LEE M. COOPER

As Ragmar grunted angrily, he pushed down on his sword and Bragore's shield began to flick and screech under the immense pressure, as it struggled to stay on. Bragore then kicked Ragmar's already injured knee out from under him, enabling him to roll backwards and detract his shield. He followed this up by throwing some small darts out from his other gauntlet, which Ragmar managed to block with his sword, using its width as a shield of his own.

Then, Ragmar swung up his mighty blade, missing Bragore's chin by a margin so small, it knicked a hair off from his chin! Bragore, visibly panicked, decided to try and use his surroundings to his advantage. Over the edge of the suspended bridge, was a thirty-foot drop into a pit of spikes. However, Ragmar had other ideas and decided he was sick of his opponent's speed getting the better of him, and so grabbed Bragore by the throat and lifted him off of the floor. As he was about to throw him over the edge, Bragore managed to hold onto his arm in a makeshift armbar type manoeuvre and pull him down using his own momentum against him. In doing so however, his legs were badly cut by his enemies' body lasers, protruding from his body armour.

Nevertheless, as Ragmar tumbled over the edge with a shocked cry of combined anger and surprise, he grabbed onto Bragore's leg at the last moment, as they both now clinged onto the edge of the walkway for dear life! Bragore, visibly losing his grip to the sheer heavy weight of Ragmar pulling him down, had to think fast before they both fell.

Might & Magic

The crowd's gasped in anticipation of what would happen next.

Ragmar having dropped his sword before he fell, still managed to hold onto his mace in his other hand. He swung it upwards in one last ditch attempt to take his opponent with him.......Bragore saw it coming.....and with one last feat of strength, he managed to activate the shield from his gauntlet.

Briefly letting go with one hand to block the incoming mace, it was timed to perfection and bounced backwards into Ragmar's face. The protruding lasers pierced into his face, killing him instantly with his own weapon. His grip released, as his lifeless body plummeted and was impaled gruesomely in the pit of spikes below.

There was a silence as Bragore clambered back onto the bridge, and after a brief moment.....the crowds erupted once more in a bloodthirsty cheer!

The King rose from his seat and applauded Bragore, so too did the KingsGuard. Unsurprisingly, Kain seemed to take a strange excitement from it in particular, shouting 'bravo, bravo'!

Imperial aids came and helped carry off an injured Bragore, to heal before his next match.

'AND NOW, A BRIEF INTERVAL LADIES & GENTLEMEN,' the announcer's voice echoed throughout the coliseum. Max was seated backstage downstairs, having just watched the opening round on the televiewer screen in the changing rooms.

'Impressive, very impressive' Max said nodding his head in approval and clapping, as Bragore was carried past him, to a healing capsule.

BY LEE M. COOPER

'Starheart! What are you doing here? Are you that eager to end up like that poor old Ragmar?' another familiar voice came from behind Max.

'You've got to be kidding me. Don't tell me you've entered as well, Jarrel'?

Jarrel walked up and patted him on the back, with a warm but concerned smile on his face.

'Listen buddy. Moranna told me you was entering, I know you have your reasons, so I won't try and talk you out of say, oh I don't know…. doing something stupid, ha ha. I just wanted to come down and say…..well, good luck.'

'Thanks. I do have my reasons…. but I also have a strategy. People are going to take notice Jarrel, and I'm going to bring the Starheart name back to the forefront of this empire.'

'Well I hope you do, for your sake! You better hurry up mate, I think your match is up next!'

Looking back across to the televiewer, the names and pictures of the upcoming round two opponents appeared.

In the King's royal box, Onix and Thamir were in conference.

'Another brutal showing by Bragore I see, it will take someone exceptional to break his winning streak it would seem' Onix said.

'Maybe…. And maybe, there is someone among the ranks this year who can do just that'

'Oh, and who might that be?' enquired Onix.

Thamir lifted his brow and replied, 'Well I have a feeling your about to see' he spoke as he pointed down towards the battle bridge.

Might & Magic

'LADIES & GENTLEMEN, PLEASE TAKE YOUR SEATS! ROUND TWO IS ABOUT TO GET UNDERWAY!' the announcement came.

'Well, if it will be anything like round one, then I suspect we will be in for a treat indeed. It appears this year, that we may have quite the pick of great talent to join the empire,' said the King eagerly.

'Indeed my King, however I have a feeling that before the end......the finalist, whoever they may be, may have quite the mountain to climb before the end,' sneered Kain with a grin.

'Sometimes Kain, I would question what exactly runs through your mind. Then again, I do not think I wish to know,' replied King Gorak.

'EVERYBODY, ARE YOU READY FOR ROUND TWO?'

The crowd returned a triumphant cheer 'BRING IT ON! BRING IT ON!' the cheers came once more.

'THEN WITHOUT FURTHER ADO, LET'S MEET CONTESTANT NUMBER ONE....'

BY LEE M. COOPER

Chapter 12: Round Two

'He comes to us from Kavlos itself, that's right ladies & gentlemen, we have a hometown hero in our midst!'

Might & Magic

'WALK THE BRIDGE! WALK THE BRIDGE! Again came the crowd, making their demands known.

'Representing the great empire of Kavlos, HE.......IS....... SERGEANT MAX....STAAARRRRRHHHEEAAAARRRTTTTTTTT!'

Although Max had been in many battles, he had never done anything quite like this before. His heart banged in his chest, his hands trembled slightly as the doors in front of him slid open and the smoke began to clear into the arena air. He stepped forward onto the battle bridge walkway to enormous roars from the crowd. They didn't often see a hometown hero participating, especially one within the empire already. Not to mention that many also already knew the heritage of the name, Starheart.

As he gazed around and forced a nervous smile to the crowds, bloodstains still lay on the ground in front him. Max took a deep breath as he laid eyes upon the gritty, red stains and then continued to turn and wave to the crowds.

'And now, contender number two! He comes to us from parts unknown, but this mysterious combatant claims to be a knight of Omeria! He's known in his land as 'The Just'.......'

'Wait, where have I heard that name before......' Max thought.

'HE......IS.....SHADOWSTORM!'

At that moment, from out of the smoky doorway at the other side of the bridge, the clanking of rusty old armour was heard, walking its way closer. A rather large, bulky shaped man emerged, shouting what sounded like his own praises.

BY LEE M. COOPER

'Yes! Yes! People of Kavlos, it is I.... Shadowstorm the Just! Look upon greatness before you, I am here from lands afar, to show you all real power'!

'You have got to be kidding me?' Max said, in an unimpressed tone.

'WHAT?! Who goes there? No......it's you! The scallywag from the bar! Oh, I shall enjoy teaching you a lesson young man. I will truly show you the power of a just & noble knight'!

Max shook his head, wondering if this man opposite him was for real. In any case, they both walked to the centre of the bridge and gave a traditional bow to the King above.

The King once again, signalled in approval, before officially opening the round.

'Begin'!

Max shouted across to the heavily girthed man, to try and appeal to him and avoid any needless bloodshed.

'Listen rusty, we don't have to do this. I don't wish to hurt you. Just yield, and you can go back to wherever it is you came from, still in one piece. Ok'?

Shadowstorm huffed, then closed his rusty, worn helmet visor down. Though he didn't appear to Max to be any particular kind of threat, the sword he carried did. As Shadowstorm held his sword sheath with one hand, he used the other to firmly grip the hilt and then with a dash.... he lunged forward with great speed. He pulled out the sword and aimed at Max with a lightning-fast upwards swipe, straight towards his face. Max was rattled. He threw himself back in shock, as he was not expecting such a large man, looking the way he did, to be so agile!

Might & Magic

Shadowstorm laughed under his helmet with a gruff, deep chuckle. To even the odds, Max although seemingly unarmed, reached out his right hand and furnished his green-hued katana, made from pure energy. In his other hand he conjured a matching green shield and stood in a fighting stance. Then, he charged back at him with a jumping spin attack of his own. To add a little more sting to the attack, he also used a push of energy upon contact with Shadowstorm.

The force knocked him back so hard; he bounced off of the steel door he entered out of, and lay on the floor, temporarily winded.

'Yield rusty! You don't know what you're getting into....'

'Ack, coff, garrrgh' he spluttered, coughing as he tried to regain his breath and composure. He stood back up, onto his feet and brought his blade to his shoulder in an attacking stance. His blade in contrast to the rest of him, was exceptionally clean and razor sharp. Just then, he did something most unexpected to Max.... he squeezed the grip and the long, shining blade was suddenly emblazoned with a blue fire!

'What the....... are you a magic caster'? Max asked in surprise.

'Hah! A type of magic you will never have seen in these parts,' Shadowstorm laughed. Then he slammed down his sword, with a great force. Though Max was able to dodge to one side with relative ease, the force that came down behind it was so great, that it caused a minor tremor which caused Max to fall to one knee. Dust even fell off from underneath the bridge with the force. Below the battle bridge in this round, instead of a pit of spikes, now lay an open flowing river of lava!

The two could feel the heat rising very quickly after only a minute or two. Max rammed his opponent with his shield, Shadowstorm couldn't block all of it in time with his sword, and so tripped as he was pushed back. Max followed this up with a stabbing thrust of his energy blade, which fortunately for Shadowstorm, went straight over his head. Shadowstorm then quickly rolled onto his back and kicked Max's feet out from under him. This also knocked off his magic weapons, due to the break in his concentration.

'Ha! Shadowstorm the Just, loses to no man'! He shouted in a boast of self-confidence.

Max then executed a backwards roll to one knee, his eyes began to glow with the same green hue of his weapons, his hands were now clenched into fists and were burning with a green flame as he began to shake. And then.... he smashed his fists into the bridge underneath him, with a scream of rage.

The floor started to crack below them, and Shadowstorm struggled to get his footing as he jumped to grab onto a piece of metal, hanging from the side of one door. Max now powered down his green hue as he needed to avoid pieces of the bridge that fell away beneath him. He jumped backwards with a rather flashy somersault and landed unharmed, as pieces of the bridge began to fall away.

The crowd roared with excitement! The announcer then came back on over the speakers.

Might & Magic

'WOW! Ladies and gentlemen, we are indeed having a treat today, although those damages WILL most likely, be coming from the taxpayers!'

'BOOOOOO' the crowd then jeered.

Shadowstorm clambered back onto a safe part of the bridge from the metal bar he was hanging onto.

'Hah, huff......huff.........it would appear that I, Shadowstorm 'The Just,' may have taken you for granted you young reprobate. However, I shall now remedy that mistake. No more games......'

Shadowstorm then raised his sword in all it's blazing, fiery glory and began to charge towards Max. Having a split second to react, Max held out both hands and imbued them with all the green, flaming magic he could muster throughout his body. As Shadowstorm's blade came down, Max caught it between his hands!

'WHA......WHAT IS THIS CHEAP TRICK?! NOBODY HAS EVER STOPPED THE FLAMING BLADE OF THE EAST'! Cried out Shadowstorm in utter shock!

Max then broke the blade between his hands, as though it were nothing more than a stick. Horrified still, Shadowstorm fell to the floor, lifting his visor.

'Now 'Shadowstorm, The Just'......one final time, do you yield'? he asked.

'I........I do......' Shadowstorm relented, with an utterly defeated tone.

'WELL, LADIES & GENTLEMEN. IT SEEMS WE HAVE A FIRST SUBMISSION THIS YEAR!'

'My King, surely this is against the rules, one lives, and one must die!,' Kain burst out to King Gorak, in a show of outrage.

BY LEE M. COOPER

'Calm yourself Kain, I am King, and my ruling is absolute! Now sit down!' Gorak retorted, shutting Kain down.

'I declare, Max Starheart the winner of this round by forfeit!' The King declared. The crowd cheered with mixes of boos, as Max bowed to his King. Then, he turned to his defeated foe and held out his hand.

'I hope we now understand one another, Shadowstorm 'The Just.'

He looked up, and with a slight smile he answered.

'I think we do…. Max Starheart.'

Meanwhile, Moranna sighed a breath of relief in her spectator box.

'I shouldn't have worried lieutenant Vix, Max has always had a knack of finding his way out of a tough spot' Jarrel spoke, as he walked up beside her.

Moranna smiled back at him, before gasping at the sight of the televiewer behind him. The camera's showed the King in his royal box, being approached by an assassin of sorts from behind. The man was dressed in the same garb, as the foreign force that attacked the gate before. Dressed head to toe in dark clothes, with his face concealed. He grabbed King Gorak from behind in a chokehold and held a plasma blade to his throat.

Onix, Thamir & Kain jumped to their King's aid, as they heard him gasp behind them.

'Whoever you are, you do not know what you do'! Shouted Onix.

'Release the King immediately, or you will suffer a pain worse than a thousand deaths over….' Thamir shouted.

Might & Magic

Kain stood at the very back, silent but almost as if waiting for something. The King shouted to his guard.

'Stand down men……what…. what is it you want'

The mysterious assassin moved closer back to the edge behind him. From here, over a short wall, was a straight hundred-foot sheer drop, down to the floor at the base of the coliseum.

'What we want, is a new beginning, a new chapter in the history of Kavlos….and it starts by ending the old chapter'!

And then, the assassin sliced Gorak's throat with the plasma blade. It gave a clean, cauterised cut but a fatal one. The King fell to the ground, as Thamir raised his arms in anger. 'NOOOOOOOOOOOOOO'! He cried. Onix ran towards the assassin, but it was too late…. the assassin had jumped to his death. Seemingly dying as a martyr of sorts.

Thamir cradled the dying King in his arms, as his brothers and personal guards gathered around.

'Yo…you…. must protect….Kav……Kav…lossss. The…re……is……a…dark…. force….at…….'

Then, the King's head fell gently to the side of Thamir's arm.

The King, was dead!

'LADIES & GENTLEMEN, WE PLEASE ASK YOU TO MAKE YOUR WAY TO THE EXITS INAN ORDERLY FASHION, THE GAMES ARE SUSPENDED. I REPEAT, WE PLEASE ASK YOU TO MAKE YOUR WAY TO THE EXITS INAN ORDERLY FASHION, THE GAMES ARE SUSPENDED!' the announcer ordered, over the speakers.

The crowds were crying & screaming in panic, unsure of what had just happened. Imperial soldiers were aiding mass exits as best as they could. The KingsGuard looked at one another....

'What has happened.... who is responsible for this murder......WE WILL HAVE BLOOD'! cried Thamir, as he cradled the dead King in his arms.

Might & Magic

Chapter 13: Shroud of Darkness

Two weeks had now passed since the tragedy at the Knightfall tournament. In the absence of a King, the KingsGuard had been in power and under direct orders from the emperor. The day of King Gorak's funeral had finally come around, and outside of the Kings royal palace, a great pyre had been built. On this rarest of occasions,

BY LEE M. COOPER

this area was open to the public of Kavlos, to pay their respects to their former King. Royal guards lined the streets all throughout the city, and the KingsGuard stood at the forefront by the body of their benevolent King.

Max was among the crowds, stood in line along with other countless imperial military personnel.

'What do you think will happen now'? he asked a soldier, stood by his side.

'No one can say for sure sir, but if the rumours are true that the emperor is set to make an appearance, then maybe he can shed some light on what lies ahead I suppose,' replied the soldier.

There were candles lit all around the pyre, messages were left from adorning fans and flowers were placed by teary eyed members of the public. Once everyone gathered who was due to be in attendance, an imperial speaker stood on a balcony just above where the King lay at rest.

'People of Kavlos, please may I have your attention. On this saddest of days, I understand the confusion, sadness, grief and uncertainty that is in the air. I am sure I speak for the Empire when I say that we are all sharing those same emotions as you. We all shared a love for our King, though his reign was not always an easy one, he persevered time and time again on many occasions. His KingsGuard Onix, Thamir & Kain stand with us today, in solidarity and to show support to our fallen King. However, they are also here to show support to the new leadership moving forward. In fact, he is here to speak to all of Kavlos here and now, himself.'

Might & Magic

The people whispered amongst themselves, uncertain of what the imperial speaker would say next. Would the emperor really, finally show himself? What would he have to say, they wondered.

'Please ladies & gentlemen, aid me in welcoming our noble emperor'!

As the speaker stood aside and bowed, the emperor himself in the flesh, finally appeared on the balcony in front of them. The ranks of the empire saluted and bowed their heads in unison at his presence, and the members of the general public gasped. They could hardly believe their eyes. Many didn't know what to make of the emperor, as he was always away from the public eye. Many more thought him a mere made up character, invented by the empire.

Alas however, Malvik truly did stand before his kingdom. He wore his usual bright silver armour, adorned with fine gems & crystals. His silver circlet of pure white gold, with a brilliant purple amethyst diamond, was also sat atop his head. He also wore a long dark blue cloak, which was fastened to his shoulder plates by golden tassels and was furnishing a tall, silver sceptre of sorts. Atop the sceptre, lay a mysterious crystal-clear orb. Although seemingly dormant, it looked as though it had some purpose, though what exactly was not obviously clear. He waved to the masses before him, with a gentle gesture. Then he spoke.

'My dear brothers & sisters of Kavlos. I must first apologise that I have not been more present in the past. However, I have never wanted to take charge over the incredible rule of our dear former King and friend, King Gorak. It deeply saddens me to be here, under these most

BY LEE M. COOPER

dire of circumstances however, and rest assured, I share all of your grief and uncertainty here today. It is a fact, that as far as we know, the late King had no heir to inherit the important duties of the day to day ruling of Kavlos. With that being said, it is with a heavy heart.... that I......your emperor Malvik, forthwith will maintain full ruling of the empire. And yes, I appreciate that this unfortunately, also spells the abolishment of a royal line.'

Cries from the crowd rang out loud, chants and boos too.

'You cannot! Kavlos has ruled under a royal line for generations!'

'There must be some other way! It has been tradition for a millennia!'

Soldiers carried off nay sayers and anyone that vocally oppressed the decision.

'I understand all of your concerns but please, rest assured, I will do my best to rule as justly as King Gorak and his line did before me. It is also with great sadness and regret, that as of this moment, I am officially disbanding the KingsGuard. Thamir, Onix and Kain will now serve under me directly. In the coming weeks, you will notice various changes I will be implementing into the day to day running of the city. However for now, I do not want this news to detract from why we are all here today. Let us all now pray, as we light the city beacons and send King Gorak to the halls of his great forefathers!'

Malvik then signalled to several archers, who, as in great tradition, fired off a flurry of flaming arrows into the pyre. King Gorak lay still, as the flames engulfed his body, and

Might & Magic

the last remnants of Kavlos' royal family……. vanished forever.

Once the procession was over and the masses started to break away, Max made his way up some stairs, away from the crowds. At the top lay a rather contemplative view, looking up at the royal palace, even far above that lay the emperor's citadel. Max suddenly realised, whether it was because the emperor had come down to speak or for some other reason…. but the cities entire magic barrier had been dropped. For the first time in his life, he could see the natural sky over Kavlos, with his own eyes. Far below, he noticed that others began to notice it too, as they pointed in astonishment.

It certainly was a day with a lot to take in for many people, be it ordinary citizens going about their everyday life, or soldiers within the empire. Everyone was affected in some way from this day forwards. Whether that was in a good way or not, remained yet to be seen.

Daydreaming always was something Max could never break the habbit of, as he mused what will happen now. To him, his friends, his family, his career even.

Thwack!

Max suddenly jolted back into reality, as a long, dark staff of sorts, slapped him gently in the back.

'What the…… can I help you, old man?' he said to the shadowy figure stood behind him.

'Ha ha, that depends. I think it is more I, who could possibly help you, young man.'

The shadowy figure then took his hood down, revealing his face. He seemed friendly enough to Max, but it did get the better of his curiosity as to what he meant.

BY LEE M. COOPER

'Max Starheart, if I'm not mistaken? Your master Thamir has spoken of you before, great potential but a bit of a daydreamer ha, ha. My name, is Halgore.........and I have a story to tell you, regarding your emperor Malvik!'

Several hours passed, into evening. And Halgore had spent those hours explaining his past, his chance meeting with Thamir, his meeting with the late King and also most importantly, divulging all he knew about Malvik.

'So Max, now you know how Malvik came to be. And as King Gorak expressed shortly before his untimely death, there is suspicion in the air, and I sense foul play at work here,' Halgore said, as he cupped his drink, in the corner of a small pub of the lower city levels.

'What about Thamir, does he know your still here? If the emperor finds out your alive and here, do you think he will come looking for you?' asked Max, also taking a swill of his beer.

'Oh I suspect he would indeed have quite the shock. However, I do not see that he believes I pose as any kind of threat to him. And indeed he would be correct. What I do know however, is that whatever he learned the day Thamir, Onix & Kain took him in, could be dangerous in his undoubtably unstable mind.'

'What do you mean? Unstable mind?'

'Well, you see. He is for all intents and purposes, a normal human that has lived for many thousands of years, with unnaturally long life. To boot, he has spent most of his days secluded in that tower, perhaps conspiring for the day he could come to absolute power. That day has come, Max. And what do you suppose, all of that power and all of

Might & Magic

that time alone, could do to one's mind hmm?' said Halgore.

'Thamir told me, of a prophecy he thought Malvik was destined to fulfil. Apparently though, the prophecy seemed to have been, shall we say, two-sided.'

'I'm, I'm sorry. Prophecy? Two-sided? How do you mean?' Max asked with a confused frown, as he scratched his head.

'Thamir spoke of a prophecy, that he and his brothers were destined to see come to fruition. The prophecy of one who would bring about an everlasting peace to Omeria. However, long after initially thinking that Malvik was that one, Thamir learned a horrible twist of fate. He learned that the prophecy, also could be misinterpreted to bring about the end of Omeria!'

Max paused for a moment, and stared at his beer as though it was a mile away into the distance, then he stooped back into his seat.

'And you think that now he may be the one to bring about this……end?'

'I do not know; we will be able to tell a lot from his next moves. But with the disbandment of the KingsGuard and his immediate appointment of himself as absolute ruler, seems somewhat ill fated if you ask me, my boy.'

'So what do you propose we do? No offense, but I'm a sergeant mage and you're an old man?' Max replied.

'Ha! I may be old, but this dog still has a few tricks up his sleeve yet, my boy. Listen, Thamir has told me, that he & Onix sense something terrible brewing, about the emperor. Especially since King Gorak died. The assassination, the recent attack. It all seems too much to be a coincidence, particularly when Kavlos has known peace for hundreds of years.'

Max rubbed his chin, as though deep in a suspicious thought, at Halgore's point. He couldn't exactly argue, everything he had said up until now was true.

'Thamir has a plan, he asked us to meet him. Tomorrow night after sundown, at the highest peak outside of the city gates. Do your loyalties lie with the emperor and his new empire, or with your former King, and the path to finding out the truth?'

As Max pondered for a second, he then answered with a determined look.

'My loyalties, like my dad's did, lie with the true ruler of Kavlos. They lie with the King!'

The next afternoon, Max had used an imperial hover bike to leave the city and arrived at the foot of the mountain Halgore spoke of. Although the kingdom of Kavlos was a mountainous region, there was no mistaking the particular peak of which he spoke of. It was an eerily shaped mountain, almost gothic and somewhat sinister by sight. It had many sharp, tall spires that would be difficult to navigate. However, it culminated in the highest peak, many fathoms above. It had a nickname, 'The Devil's Peak.'

Max scoffed to himself at the irony, that he would be meeting a mysterious old man and a former KingsGuard, to discuss amongst a secret committee, at such a place. He parked his bike at the foot of the mountain, behind a secluded, unassuming range of rocks and began to make his ascent. The sun had only just started to go down, but

Might & Magic

he knew it would take him two or three hours to reach the summit. And daylight wasn't on his side. He knew he needed to be quick, yet careful. Many before him, had fallen prey to these mountain ranges and they were to be treated with the upmost respect. Anything less, could mean losing his life quite easily to them.

As he climbed carefully, he remembered his climbing skills from the imperial academy, which came in quite useful. Also, standard issue imperial uniform, included special retractable spikes within the boots, which could be used to aid in such activities. Max found these quite useful, as he also used a grapple rope, to help reach the harder areas with greater ease. As he climbed, he couldn't help but wonder who else may be waiting at the top. Could it possibly be a trap of some sort? What would be discussed? How could Halgore climb this? How would he get back down? Hopefully Thamir may be able to teleport him back to the bottom, as long as he asked nicely, he thought!

Two and a half hours later, as the sun wasn't far off of the horizon now, Max had finished climbing the most difficult parts of the mountain some fifty or so minutes ago. From here, an off beaten winding path was able to take him the rest of the way to the summit. Just as he came upon the final areas of the rocky range, he could hear voices coming from the top.

'People talking, must be Thamir and whoever else I'm supposed to be meeting,' Max thought to himself.

As he finally reached the top, it appeared as though Halgore was indeed a man of his word. There, standing in front of a crimson sunset as it glistened off of his brilliant

BY LEE M. COOPER

red armour, was Thamir. A small camp had been set up just across the way, in a more sheltered area. It seemed some or all of the other members of this meeting had plans to stay the night at least. Just in front of the sheltered area, lay a small campfire. Halgore was by it, looking as though he was cooking something at the end of his staff over it. Behind him, lay his ever-trusty friend and steed, Indi.

'Gwwarrhhkkk!' Indi squawked, as she noticed the presence of new company.

'Ah, Max my boy. Good to see you, I'm glad you were able to tackle this difficult terrain. That in itself, shows great strength of character!' said Halgore.

Max nodded and replied.

'Indeed, I haven't faced a climb that tough since…. well ever! And how did you get up here anyway?'

'Ha ha! As I said my boy, I have a few tricks left in me yet!'

Thamir then walked over to greet Max and placed a hand on his shoulder.

'Max Starheart, thank you for coming. I am sorry to have dragged you out this far, but the emperor has eyes everywhere. Unfortunately, that includes my brother Kain. However we have matters to discuss of the gravest importance.' Whenever Thamir spoke in such a dreaded way, it sent shivers down Max's spine.

'Please have a seat, now that we are all here'

At that moment, some shadowy figures that were sat inside the sheltered area, walked outside and came into Max's field of view.

Might & Magic

'Jarrel! Moranna! And....... Shadowstorm?!' Max shouted in utter surprise.

'Yes, these are so far, the only others I could rally to hear my cause,' Thamir said.

'You didn't think you was the only one in the empire, loyal to the King did ya mate?' Jarrel asked, with a smile as he walked over and patted Max on the arm.

'And after I saw the change in the King, and his mental illness begin to set in, I knew something worrying was afoot, Max. I heard rumours through my sources, that Master Thamir was looking for likeminded people, to attend a secret council and listen to his plea. So here I am,' explained Moranna.

'And what's your story, rusty?'

'HA! I have travelled from far away lands. And though my story is one for another day, I have nowhere else to go. And I, Shadowstorm 'The Just,' am ever one for an adventure! My people have always respected the King of these lands, and so it would be my honour, to help aid in any way I can!'

'I see, well then do not let me hold you up any longer master Thamir, please continue,' said Max.

'It has been no secret to the KingsGuard, that emperor Malvik has long sought to overthrow the late King. This of course, was not public knowledge. And I suspect only me, and my kin knew of it within the whole empire. Now I have no evidence, of any crimes committed against the late King Gorak. Though I feel that his assassination was orchestrated in some way. I suspect my brother Kain knows more about it than he is willing to divulge, but alas, I feel it is my duty to set things right. I have intel that the emperor plans to move against the other continents of Omeria.'

'But if this was all orchestrated, master Thamir, what purpose has the emperor to initiate a war on any peaceful neighbouring states?' Moranna asked with great concern.

'A good question Lieutenant mage, I am unsure exactly what his motives for this mindless act of war seem to be. However from close council with him in the past, he seems more and more obsessed over the years, with fulfilling what he believes his prophecy to be. Unfortunately, it appears that he believes, to bring about a global peace, first means conquering it, as its dictator.'

Thamir solemnly bowed his head, as though saying the words aloud, brought shame to him.

'If you think Kain is in league with him, what about master Onix?' said Max.

'He, like I, is well aware of the emperor's intentions. However, he has been tasked, by the emperor himself, to help amass a war party. He is only doing so right now, so as to not arouse suspicion, and to buy me some time.'

'So what do you suggest master? If the emperor has gone as mad as you say, what chance do we few have?' said Jarrel.

At this point, Halgore looked up and interrupted.

'That is why, we must head to the eastern continent first. That is where Onix has advised he will strike first, since nearly all of this continent, already falls under the kingdom of Kavlos' jurisdiction.'

'THE EASTERN CONTINENT!' Shadowstorm shouted.

Might & Magic

'Yes Shadowstorm. If what we have been told is correct, then it appears that Malvik will be looking to strike the next most dominant military force in Omeria. That would point to the Eastern continent, and the Kingdom of Avaloria. He would see it as a threat, but one we could use to our advantage,' Thamir responded to him.

'I see....' Shadowstorm said, looking away.

'Is there some problem with heading towards Avaloria, Shadowstorm?' asked Moranna.

'NO! I mean.... well. Hmph, I do not like to speak of my past but the Kingdom of Avaloria is where I am from. In fact, the capital Avaloria itself, is where I was stationed as a knight. Though.......I'm not exactly welcome there anymore,' he replied shunning away in embarrassment.

'Listen, whatever the reason, I'm sure they would welcome you if you were helping to bring news on an incoming invasion, Shadowstorm,' said Max.

'I assume if we do this, we will be outcasts. Traitors to the Kingdom of Kavlos. Banished forever,' Jarrel asked Thamir.

'Yes, there is no easy way to say it. Once we go missing, there will be search parties out for us, no doubt. The emperor plans to act swiftly, Onix tells me he leaves with his army in two days. I suggest if any of you have any goodbyes to say, now will be the time. If you are willing to find the courage to accompany me on this perilous journey, we will take the ex-KingsGuard airship, the 'Justice.'

'Wow, THE Justice? Isn't she the fastest airship Kavlos has?' Max asked Thamir, as his eyes lit up with excitement.

'Yes, she is, or at least was. I know the emperor has commissioned the construction of a new airship, one that has been secretly in development for some time now. I have not seen or heard of it, as he has kept it pretty close to his chest, but I suspect it will be even more powerful than the 'Justice.' And once he notices that the 'Justice' has gone without leave, they will attempt to track us.'

The small band of various warriors, all looked around at each other, wondering if anyone was having second thoughts. Yet after a few moments, no one stepped forward.

'Very well, if there are no further questions then we are all in agreement here. Meet me at the royal palace, in two days, after sundown. Our best chance to slip away unnoticed, will definitely be at night. I have authority to get us into the hangar, underneath the palace. With a bit of luck and a following wind, we may just make it out in one piece!' said Thamir.

'Well, I guess if we were going to do this, there isn't a finer grouping of skill and courage that I'd rather be a part of,' said Max.

'Indeed, this will no doubt be a dangerous mission, but also a noble one. I am with you master Thamir,' Moranna firmly said.

'Of course, I can't let Max Starheart have all the fun! Count me in,' confirmed Jarrel.

'Ha ha, well isn't this becoming a fine band. I have never flown by airship, so I am very intrigued. Also, stopping the invasion is obviously very important also ha ha,' Halgore nodded in agreement.

Might & Magic

Shadowstorm, still quiet and unsure of himself, at last relented.

'WHERE NOBILITY AND JUSTICE GO, SO TOO DOES SHADOWSTORM 'THE JUST,' HAHA! I TOO SHALL JOIN YOU!'

Thamir looked around with pride and a gentle smile. He crossed his arm across his chest and gave a slight bow.

'I am honoured, my fellow warriors to be amongst such honourable spirits as yourselves. However even if we manage to get to Avaloria, we must convince their King that we are not spies or tricksters of any kind. And not only that...'

Thamir turned and looked over the cliff edge, towards the burning horizon.

'They are not the warmest of hosts......'

Chapter 14: The Course of Justice

She looked puzzled at Max, as though she couldn't quite understand why this duty fell to him.

'I'm sorry Max, don't get me wrong, I'm very proud of all you've accomplished and your sense of pride & duty towards Kavlos. I just don't see why you feel you have to

Might & Magic

take part in this. If the empire find's out you're a part of divulging top-secret information to the enemy...' Martha said before she was abruptly interrupted by Max.

'Mum! I've told you, Avaloria are NOT the enemy!' he sighed.

'I'm sorry mum, I don't expect you to entirely understand. And if anyone other than master Thamir himself had told me the things he did, I'd struggle to believe it myself too.'

Martha poured more tea into Max's cup, as they sat around a roaring log fire in her living room. She looked up at a photo on the wall, of her late husband.

'You know, your father also did a lot of things in the line of duty that I never understood too,' she smiled. 'But I always knew better than to question his ways. How I do miss him, Max. You remind me so much of him, headstrong, responsible and always putting the kingdom first before anything. I guess you've made up your mind, and far be it from me to try and talk you out of it. I know better,' Martha said.

Max cradled his cup, looking down, and he then smiled somewhat sombrely.

'Thanks mum. I don't know how long I'll be gone, but I promise I will call you whenever I get the first chance.'

'When do you leave?'

'Tonight, a couple of hours from now.'

'I take it you're crossing by boat then?'

'Well......not exactly. But the less you know, the better mum, trust me!' Max nervously joked.

BY LEE M. COOPER

'Oh dear. Well please, just promise me you'll be careful and don't take any unnecessary risks! You know how I worry, and you're all I've got left!'

Max walked over to where his mother was sat and gave her a big hug. She reciprocated with an even tighter embrace back.

'Jeez, go easy mum ha ha. You squeeze any tighter and I'll be good for nothing at all!'

Afterwards they walked towards the front door and Max placed his hands on his mothers' shoulders, smiling warmly at her.

'I promise I'll be careful. Now I'm afraid I have to go; time is short, and the others will be waiting for me. I love you mum, hold onto this for me. I'll want it back.'

He passed her a long silver chain, with a military crest on it.

'Max…….this was your father's. He left it you?'

'Which is exactly why I'll be needing it back,' he winked at her and gave her a soft kiss on the cheek.

And then he walked out of the front door, almost reminiscent of all those years ago, when he first left to start his new life in the empire's military corps. She stood in the doorway, as she watched him walk off into the lowly lit streets and into the night. He didn't look back.

Shortly afterwards, Max began his approach towards the royal palace. He noticed that security was pretty lax, and he hadn't really run into anybody throughout town either. In a most unusual sight, for the first time that he could remember, he could almost hear a pin drop outside. He wondered at first, if this was some kind of trap. That word

Might & Magic

of their plan to steal the 'Justice,' had reached the emperor and he had something sinister planned for them. However as Max cautiously and quietly made his way up the driveway towards the main palace gates, he was somewhat shocked that he was able to walk right up, pretty much unopposed. As he arrived at the gates however, they were firmly closed and locked tight. He looked down at the nearby control panel, the light was red, signalling that they were locked. With no one around to meet him and lacking any obvious opportunities to sneak through as he had hoped for originally, he had to improvise.

Max wondered if he may be able to manipulate the control panel magically somehow, without triggering the alarm. With no key, his options were extremely limited. He slowed down his breathing and held his hands over the panel. As the green mist like power began to emerge from his palms, it started to find its way in through small cracks in the panel. This wasn't something Max had ever tried before, so he was using his instincts to guide him, and hoped for the best.

After a few seconds, a 'clichkk!' sound was heard along with an affirmative 'beep!' The light on the panel turned green and the gates began to slide open. Max couldn't believe his luck, he was in! Well almost, he still had the unenviable task of making his way into the palace itself, finding the others and high jacking a class A royal airship, all without immediately alerting security.

'Well, I've been in worse jams,' he thought.

As he snuck quietly through the gates and towards the main front double doors of the palace, he noticed they

BY LEE M. COOPER

were already open just a little. At this point it was too late to turn back now, but he had a very bad feeling about this. His main hope now, was that one of the others had already come through this way and had left it open, either accidently or in anticipation of Max arriving after. Nevertheless, he slowly and quietly began to push the door open. Inside, he could see the main hallway was well lit.

'Oh no.....this looks bad,' as a thought of dread overcame him. He glanced around the area in front of him, there were at least nine guards from what he could tell, all lay on the floor motionless. He walked over to the nearest one, reaching down for a pulse on his neck.

'Ok...ok a pulse,' he breathed a slight sigh.

To his relief, these guards at least weren't dead but rather just unconscious. He followed the trail quickly towards a door on the left. Upon opening it, their led a stairwell downwards, to a more open area. The way was clear, as Max quickly made his descent downwards. At the bottom, two great steel doors labelled 'Hangar Bay,' greeted him. They were already parted through the middle, albeit via erosion. Some acidic like magic seemed to have been the cause, it looked a powerful spell whatever the case Max thought to himself.

As he stepped through the mangled doors, he was finally into the hangar. This was a huge area, several miles in all directions as it lay far below the palace, and deep within the mountain. And before him, lay the 'Justice' in all her glory. He'd never seen her up close before, as he looked in awe at the sheer size of this one-of-a-kind airship.

Might & Magic

She was made up of a combination of a steel cockpit that hanged in suspension within the docking bay. This part was encased in thick, bullet proof glass that covered the circumference of the arrow shaped pilot's bridge. Shaped around the cockpit, was a design similar to a gaping beast's mouth, with giant fangs, so as to instil fear at its very presence. Above and to the sides, in the design of a great mythical beast, lay two gigantic arms that housed the engines, with clawed talons raising from each. These were not just a design for prestige & flamboyance, but also served as useful weapons in close quarters 'ramming' tactics in the air. Above the talons were huge propellers, furnished with blades of gold, which was a nice contrast to its deep royal blue that coated the rest of the ship. Her design was fearsome, yet agile. Battle hardened and yet a spectacle over the skies. In past skirmishes overseas, the mere sight of the 'Justice,' was more than enough to grind cities into submission.

Oddly enough, the 'Justice' was one of the rare, few aircraft that wasn't completely powered by magic essence fuel. This was, in part, due to the fact that many non-magic users in the empire would be piloting her, and this meant that any on-the-fly repairs, had to be able to be completed by ordinary mechanics. The sheer size of the ship didn't leave much room in the hangar for many others, except for a few shuttles anchored nearby.

'Starheart……you mustn't let your guard down,' said a female voice suddenly. As he slowly moved his eyes downward, a plasma bladed sword was at his throat.

'Lieutenant Vix, well if it were anyone else, I'd be worried' he said, slowly lowering the blade.

BY LEE M. COOPER

'It's good to see a friendly face around here, or rather a face at all. I was getting a little worried.'

'Indeed, master Thamir is already on board trying to get the 'Justice' prepped for take-off, as is Jarrel & Halgore. I'm afraid the mess we left behind isn't quite what I had in mind, but rather the handiwork of....'

Before Moranna could finish.

'ME! HA HA! SHADOWSTORM 'THE JUST'!

'Listen Shadowstorm, as much as I appreciate the help, I think we would benefit from a little more, shall we say, discretion. And please, can you keep your voice down, you don't need to shout everything,' replied Max.

'IYE, sorry...I...errr.... mean yes, apologies. In my country, we are a hearty folk, and we do things whichever way we must, to get the job done.' As he said this, he held firmly onto his sword by his side, it was still illuminating with a blue hue, from whatever magic spell he had put on it to cut through the huge bulk hangar doors.

'Listen, we need to focus now on getting aboard, before anyone is alerted to Shadowstorm's 'handiwork,' said Moranna. She then proceeded to lead the two up a flight of nearby steel steps, leading up and across to the boarding bridge.

As the three arrived at the 'Justices' boarding ramp, Jarrel stood in the doorway flagging them in.

'What took you so long mate, we all arrived about half an hour ago. Letting us do all the hard work eh?' he said.

'Sorry, I needed to say my goodbyes to my mother' replied Max in a sorrowful tone.

Might & Magic

'It's ok, I know how it is. You should've told her you're in safe hands with your best buddy!' Jarrel laughed.

'Ah, Max! I'm glad to see our group in finally all here in one piece!' said Halgore, walking up from inside the ship. 'If you will please all follow me, master Thamir is upstairs making preparations for our departure, and we mustn't linger any longer!'

The group walked in and closed the boarding ramp behind them. The interior was as lavish on the inside as it was impressive on the outside. As the ship was formerly commissioned by the late King and used by the KingsGuard, it was furnished with only the finest materials money could buy. Within the entrance bay, there were doors off either side. One led to a hold designed to carry either regiments of soldiers, no more than fifty or so of the most elite. Or it could double as a prisoner hold if needed. A door on the other side held crew quarters and a small living space.

Walking up the stairs led to the upper floor, here lay the main cockpit and the captain's quarters. The captain's quarters held beds for not only the captain, but up to five other high-ranking officials. The cockpit was the largest room however and was more the size of a traditional bridge. The ship could be flown by a minimum of two, but three to five was often preferred in warfare.

Thamir was sat in the main captain's chair, which faced directly ahead.

'Come, please take a seat everyone. We are just about ready for take-off. I just need to disengage the parking lock and open the hangar bay doors so we can get out of here,'

BY LEE M. COOPER

he said whilst pushing a myriad of different knobs and switches.

As Jarrel, Moranna, Max, Halgore and Shadowstorm sat down and strapped themselves in, the engines began to come to life with a roar, as they kicked out a plume of black smoke, after being sat unused for so long. The propellers started to slowly turn, Thamir turned to look over his shoulder at the others.

'Now brace yourselves, it has been quite some time since I piloted this ship so it may be slightly bumpy.'

He moved the control stick gently, trying to initiate a take-off away from the parking bay. A 'cluchunck!' noise sounded, as he struggled to pull away…something wasn't letting go of the ship.

'Ah, apologies all. I'd forgotten to disengage the parking brake,' he said.

He pushed a couple of buttons, and a green light lit up over his head, to notify this had now been detached. He once again tried to pull up and turn away slowly. This time, after a few loud creaking sounds made from the boarding bridge and a cloud of dust falling away from the holding arms, the 'Justice' finally began to move away. The next issue Thamir had, was to open the hangar bay doors which were located towards the rear of the hangar. These doors opened from the rear of the mountain it was set deep within, but once through these…. they would be home free to escape towards their destination, Avaloria.

'Gah, this is annoying. I cannot for the life of me remember where the hangar door switch is located….' Thamir said aloud, with a tone of self-irritance.

Might & Magic

Moranna walked over to Thamir, to try and aid him from the knowledge she had of the imperial shuttles she'd had experience with. She looked down at a panel in front of Thamir and flicked a switch, which then lit another over his head.

'Bingo!' she said, as she hit the final switch above. A confirmed bell sounded, as the gigantic hangar bay doors began to open, letting in the light of the stars from outside, in the night sky.

'Lieutenant Vix, most impressive!' Thamir affirmed, with an approving nod.

'Tch, I could've done that. It's just because she was the first one up,' Jarrel shrugged in his seat.

The doors took a couple of minutes to fully open wide enough, to allow the 'Justice' out. Once they were, Thamir started to move the control stick forwards but had to immediately readjust his strength. He'd forgotten how sensitive and powerful the ship was!

'Wow, please, try to aim for between the doors and not into the wall!' cried out Halgore in a slight panic.

Thamir reaffirmed the ships position and gently eased the ship out of the doors, finally out into the freedom of the open world. The 'Justice' powered out with a roar into the clear night sky, by this point it would have alerted any remaining soldiers left on patrol, amongst the castle grounds.

'At last, we made it. I have plotted the course; it will take us over the dark seas and across the border of Avaloria. According to the autopilot system, it states that we should be there by the morning,' Thamir advised.

BY LEE M. COOPER

The party breathed an air of temporary comfort, as the 'Justice' climbed into the night, with silent elation.

Back at the emperor's citadel, Malvik watched from his window, as he witnessed the 'Justice' climb towards the stars and head east, before disappearing into the clouds.

'My emperor, is this completely wise? Letting Thamir and his little band of mutinous traitors escape in the 'Justice?' Kain said lingering behind him in the shadows, of his lowly lit throne room.

Malvik sneered with a sinister chuckle to himself, he turned to face Kain with an evil grin.

'Do not worry my faithful servant, all is going to my initial designs. They will be branded as traitors to the Kingdom of Kavlos, responsible for both the attacks on the city and the assassination of the beloved King. Thamir is too dangerous to be kept alive.....especially as he is now in league with that insolent old fool, Halgore. I'm amazed the sands didn't kill him long ago, still, he is a loose end I want taken care of, Kain.'

'Of course my lord, but do you not wish me to pursue them? I could give them quite the bit of trouble amongst the skies,' he asked with a smile.

'No that won't be necessary, I have appointed Onix to follow with a battalion of my best men at first light. We will see where his loyalties truly lie.'

'I have other uses for you Kain. You will accompany me in two days' time, as we head for Avaloria. We will swoop in after Onix's initial attack and break whatever is left of their King's defences, along with Thamir's band of

Might & Magic

traitorous dog's. It is imperative that my new ship is ready by then, see to it personally Kain.'

'As you wish my lord,' Kain bowed and left the room with haste.

Emperor Malvik looked back out into the night sky. The air was quiet with an unnerving, dark atmosphere about it. He looked down to a small table beside him, on which lay the book he had been holding onto with the greatest of care for hundreds of years. The 'Book of Rebirth' sat there, withered looking. It was littered with ancient emblems and inscriptions. One side contained a face of light and hope. The other side depicted a face of great evil, with fangs of darkness and destruction about it.

'Oh Thamir, if only you understood you misguided fool. You were right all along; I AM THE ONE OF PROPHECY!'

He opened the book and placed a hand on one of the decrepit looking pages, feeling across the inscriptions with his gloved fingers. He closed his eyes and felt the words rile and stir within him; he chanted an ancient long dead language under his breath. The few torches that lit the room, flickered and turned colour to a deep red, the wind outside picked up and began to batter the balcony doors to and fro. Malvik opened his eyes, which now were ablaze with an unnatural red and yellow tone, his pupil's changed shape to a more monstrous form. The bright silver armour he usually adorned was suddenly enveloped in darkness and black. The gems turned into a deep red and burned within with an otherworldly presence, as if they were alive! His face wrinkled with pulsing veins underneath his skin, and his long golden hair turned to ashen black. Even his once glistening, beautiful sword turned to shadow, and became reborn as the guard turned into live, demon like claws and the blade smoked with an evil essence about it. And his circlet atop his head, turned into a wreath of flame.

This was dark magic of the most ancient kind, not of this world. This was the true power that Malvik had worshipped for so long. It spoke to his mind and blackened his soul. He had truly made the ultimate sacrifice.

He said one more thing to himself that night, as though something else were living within him. A possessed, haunting voice spoke through him...

'TO CREATE PEACE AND PROSPERITY, THE WORLD MUST FIRST BURN ASUNDER IN DARKNESS AND CHAOS......'

Might & Magic

Chapter 15: Thunderous Pursuit

Onix stood in the same hangar, where the 'Justice' was anchored mere hours ago. A new day was dawning, and he'd been given his orders. He had rallied a battalion of the emperors' best troops, consisting of armed soldiers, magic casters and everything in between.

BY LEE M. COOPER

He knew he had bought Thamir some time to try and warn Avaloria, and he wished he were with them. His hope now would be that Avaloria would either be battle ready enough to deflect the emperors incoming attack, or that he himself could somehow stop Malvik.

'This is wrong,' he thought.

If he were to try and defeat Malvik himself, he would need all the information Kain knew about him to gain the advantage. That would be difficult, his time was limited and Kain was nowhere to be seen. No doubt the emperor had some other sinister tasks afoot for him, he thought. Of what shuttles and aircraft were left to him, none were any match for the 'Justice,' even if they could outnumber it ten to one.

'Soldiers of the empire, heed my words to you now,' he began to speak to the crowd.

'The forces we have been tasked with finding, are in possession of the 'Justice' airship, as you are all now aware. With what we have here left at our disposal, we will not be able to overcome such an airship. However, what we can do, is buy enough time with a distraction. A distraction long enough, until the emperor himself and master Kain arrive. He has commissioned a new ship, one which we are told, that will be more than enough to rival the 'Justice.'

Soldiers looked around at each other at this news, they could scarcely believe anything would be able to rival it.

'Sir, with all due respect...we would need one hell of a ship to rival her?' one man shouted.

Might & Magic

'I understand your concern soldier, but rest assured I will not needlessly send this party to their deaths. We must trust in the emperor's words.'

Onix had to keep morale up, even if he scarcely believed the words he spoke, himself.

'With that being said, time grows short, and the fugitives already have quite the head start on us. Now, to your ships all!' he spoke with a salute to his men.

As the men ran to their shuttles, Onix felt a heavy burden, a deep regret that things had come to this after so many years. Nevertheless, he had to act quickly if he had any chance to stall the emperor. With no sign of Kain for the time being to try and dissuade him, his only other option was to take the next fastest ship available to him in the hangar and head towards Avaloria.

Meanwhile, Kain had left Kavlos the evening before on the emperors' orders. The ship he spoke of being commissioned, had been in development secretly for years. Malvik had planned ahead for this day and had long ago rallied the best mechanical and engineering minds of Kavlos to build him the ultimate weapon. Following co-ordinates that Malvik had left him, he had taken a small aircraft and was on his way to the top-secret location.

It lay on a small, unmapped island just off the northern coast. Even Kain was unaware of the remote location's existence, even with all his years of knowledge on the land. After several hours of travel, he finally reached the co-ordinates, as he hovered over the waters.

'I don't see anything here, just some small rocks rising from the surface. This cannot be correct,' he said in confusion.

BY LEE M. COOPER

After a few more seconds just as he was about to leave, the water below began to part!

'What in the emperor's name……' Kain muttered in sheer bewilderment.

He now saw that the co-ordinates were correct, but this wasn't just a secret island construction yard, of sorts. Rather, it was a subterranean high-tech construction facility. Once the doors had opened and enough water had drained into the vents at either side, Kain saw that he was safe to make his descent. It appeared as though he was expected. He landed several meters below sea level, into a basic looking hangar bay and was greeted by a middle-aged man in an engineer's coat. He wore high tech goggles and held a clipboard close by his chest. Two imperial officers flanked him.

'Greeting's master Kain, I hope you didn't have too much trouble finding our somewhat, clandestine location. Though, the emperor felt that utmost secrecy be required for the task we have undertaken here. My name is Cedrick, and I am the lead engineer here. If you will please follow me, I understand time is short, however I think you and the emperor, will be most pleased with our progress,' he then walked with a quick pace as Kain followed.

They walked through a simple door at the end of the room, which led to a slim, lightly lit yet simple hallway. Kain couldn't help but notice that the place had seemed purpose built for this one project but wondered just how long this had been here. Once they arrived at the end of the hallway, Cedrick stopped and turned abruptly.

Might & Magic

'Now beyond this door, lies a site that no one from the surface world has seen before, except the emperor. You have the honour master Kain, of being the first after him. Our engineers were hand-picked by the emperor himself many years ago, to construct a ship to his specifications. We have worked closely with him to make the most powerful aircraft ever built, even more so than the 'Justice'!

He opened the door, as they walked through, Kain slowly looked up. Indeed what he saw was at least twice as big as the 'Justice'!

'Incredible! I have never seen a ship so big! It must be a third the size of the city at least!' Kain said in astonishment.

'heh heh, quite my lord. You see, many of the engineers here had family before them, that worked on the 'Justice.' These are the best in the world at what they do. And so I give to you......

'The Kingslayer!'

Kain looked at the engineer with a sarcastic look.

'An ironic name?'

'Heh heh, let us say though our great emperor devised the name, he is not without a sense of humour it would seem,' Cedrick said.

'Indeed it would not,' Kain cautiously agreed. There was something about the engineer that he did not entirely trust. He turned back to look at the hulking brute of a battleship in amazement. Cedrick intervened with excitement, as though he couldn't wait to explain all about it.

BY LEE M. COOPER

'Let me educate you master Kain, in our grand project here. This is the first ever destroyer class airship, built for total annihilation of its targets. It has a multitude of different armaments, including but not limited to.... blasters, homing missile launchers, plasma disc projectors, flamethrowers and a couple of other surprises. Also, unlike the 'Justice,' it is able to be powered with magic fuel essence, as per the emperors' request.'

To look at, its design was clearly mammoth in size and painted jet black. Unlike the 'Justice,' it did not have any kind of mythical animal traits in its design, more just constructed with warfare in mind. In shape, it was sleek for its size, with a more streamlined look and many smooth curves for speed. The 'Kingslayer' was fairly flat looking, all compartments being on one level. It had room enough to hold around five thousand troops with ease. It had a cockpit at the front, with four huge engines either side, towards the rear it had a long steel tail that stated its namesake along it.

'Well let us just hope Avaloria doesn't try to put up a fight,' Kain said.

Aboard the 'Justice,' it was now early morning the following day after the hijacking, and spirits were hopeful.

'Master Thamir,' said Jarrel in the cockpit.

'Forgive my possible stupidity, but I always wondered....... if the KingsGuard were always able to teleport around, why did you just not teleport to Avaloria to warn its people?'

'Ha, not such a stupid question as you may think young Mr Jones. Yes, we are able to teleport, however only

Might & Magic

across short distances. The eastern continent lies far beyond any of our physical reach,' Thamir explained back to him with a smile.

In the captains' quarters towards the rear of the ship, Moranna and Max were seated looking out of the small window, at the sea below. The day was bright but with a few clouds over the dark sea.

'It's been hours now, and still no sign of land or of anyone following our tail. It's a strange feeling, kind of feels like we are in limbo......don't you think?' asked Max.

'Hmmm. I'm just happy that we're safe, for now,' replied Moranna.

'Listen, I don't mean to pry......but don't you have any family you left behind in Kavlos? And I always thought you were career orientated. What will you do, if we succeed in this mission?'

'I have no family. I was an orphan. The empire took me in from an early age, once they realised that I showed great magical potential. The empire is all I've ever really known. But if we survive this, I can only hope to offer my services to rebuilding Kavlos, a better Kavlos. One the King would've wanted, either that or I die trying,' she said with a straight, determined face.

Max looked at her with a slim smile.

'Well let's hope it doesn't come to that.'

'HA! I mean, ahem.....may I join you two?,' Shadowstorm abruptly said as he wandered into the room.

'Please,' Max said offering up a spare chair.

His armour clinked and clanked as he strode across the room, letting out a moan, 'hummpphhh,' as he sat down.

BY LEE M. COOPER

'I felt I needed to elaborate on my past in Avaloria, before we arrive,' he said.

'I was once a knight captain, serving in the King's army there. It was my ultimate goal and privilege to serve since I was a boy. Then one day, about six years ago, we were attacked by a renegade mercenary group. We were unsure of what their motive was, but it was my job as captain, to make sure no one breached the walls of our city......'

Shadowstorm looked down and stared at the floor, as he continued with his story.

'But.......one was a magic user. I tried to stop him, but......a mother and child were killed. They were engulfed in a ball of fire, by one of the mercenaries. I WAS TOO LATE! I ran over and cut down the brigand shortly after. Though they threw a fire ball at me too as I charged them. I survived, though my armour was a little worse for wear afterwards. Following the assault, for my failure to save those poor innocent civilians, the King cast me out of his service and banished me, never to return to Avaloria.'

Moranna spoke up.

'What? That's absurd, you tried your best and you got punished for it,' Moranna angrily replied, with a raised voice.

'Hmph, indeed I know it may seem strange to you. However that is the way of our culture. We either achieve victory.....or die trying.'

'I'm sorry Shadowstorm, I didn't realise you had such a rough ride. I am curious though, where did your magic ability come from?' asked Max.

Might & Magic

'HA! In Avaloria, our customs and magic are much different to yours in Kavlos. We worship our war god, and he gives us strength in battle. He imbues our weapons with power, to slay our foes! Which is also why I must also warn everyone, any unwarranted approach to the capital will be met with furious aggression. It is just their way; they are a very defensive nation.'

'You mentioned you were banished, what will happen if we mention that you have accompanied us? Do you think we will gain any lenience with their forces? Moranna asked.

'HA HA! Most unlikely I'm afraid. If anything, it might make matters worse. To try and return from banishment, is an offense punishable by death....' Shadowstorm nervously advised the two.

The clouds began to clear from out the viewpoint, and the beginnings of land now started to come into view. Gulls flew about, over the crashing waves upon the rocks, and a beach was now also visible.

'Everybody to the bridge, we have reached the eastern coast,' Thamir's voice spoke over the speaker.

As the group all took their allocated seats on the bridge once more, Shadowstorm advised Thamir to slow his approach.

'I think it best if we avoid surprising The King of this land, the only way we may make it to land without being attached, is if we can make radio contact and convince them that we come in peace, with important tidings.

'I agree Shadowstorm,' Thamir nodded in approval.

'This is former KingsGuard Thamir of Kavlos, aboard the 'Justice.' I have come with a small party to bring urgent news to your King. It is imperative that we are allowed permission to land, over.'

There was a deathly silence over the airwaves, as the ship hovered over the coastal line. The capital was not quite yet in view, but Thamir knew the walls didn't lie too far inland. Avaloria was well known for the best naval fleet in the world and had never been breached by sea attack in its long history. Though the ships currently lay hidden from view, Thamir was well aware that they were no doubt being closely watched.

Thamir once again repeated his plea over the radio and waited patiently, as the others looked around nervously in anticipation of a reply. After a few more painstakingly quiet moments, a reply voiced back over the radio.

'This is the Avalorian fleet, the King has not been made aware of your visit. Does your ship come alone?' the voice asked.

'That is correct. I apologise for our sudden intrusion into your lands; however time was not a luxury afforded to us at this juncture. We come with news of a great threat, the emperor of Kavlos has gone mad, he means to force an attack upon you. We must warn your King in person!' Thamir replied, with an urgency in his voice.

'.........You may approach.....slowly. If this is some kind of trap however, we WILL open fire upon you,' the voice demandingly stated back.

Thamir looked at his crew, with a look of nervous relief. He began to gently take the ship inland; within only a couple of minutes, they began to see the shape appear of the Avalorian capital city. It was a grand city, not quite the

Might & Magic

size of Kavlos, however the city lay well protected, with a great moat surrounding it. Within the moat were channels of water, these led off to various bases around the coastal line, which contained their naval fleet. A few of their best warships were always stationed nearby however, as part of their outer defences. The ships were made of a great, almost impregnable steel and were housed with many cannons, guns and launchers of various sorts.

As for Avaloria itself, it's walls elevated high up, and guns mounted it all around. Within its great walls, a few skyscrapers rose above wall level, but many of the other buildings were much smaller in size. The King's palace resided in the centre and was raised, with many grand statues surrounding it from the outside. There were also several temples dotted around the city, as it was known for its spiritual and religious beliefs, as much as for its great naval armada.

As the 'Justice' began to approach the city walls, Thamir saw a red dot on the ships radar system. A strange blinking approaching from its rear, gaining closer and closer.

A voice broke in over the communications system;

'To the 'Justice' and her crew, this is master Onix. Thamir, I implore you, for your own safety…. please stand down now. It is too late, Kain and the emperor are not far behind, and they follow with a force much worse than I.'

Thamir replied;

'My old friend, you know what we must do here, is for the greater good of Kavlos and Omeria as a whole. We cannot allow Malvik to wreak havoc on the world. We must make our stand here; we cannot run from him forever, as well you know.'

BY LEE M. COOPER

Onix was accompanied by fifty or so smaller ships. It was not a force that would be able to stop the 'Justice' or pose as too much of a threat to Avaloria for that matter. From his command chair, Onix deep down agreed all too much with Thamir. He even wished he were on the other side of this fateful predicament. As the 'Justice' and Onix's battalion were locked in a standoff, an alarmed voice radioed in over every ship in the air.

'This is the captain of the Avalorian fleet, we will NOT be made fools of! We were told only one ship was present. Prepare to feel the full force of the Avalorian fleet!'

Both the 'Justice' and Onix's battalion immediately braced for impact, as every visible weapon from the fleet below turned and pointed high up towards them. With military precision, they all shot off a salvo of cannon fire. Their weapons were some of the most renowned in all the world, and the situation became dire fast.

Thamir was quickly aided by Max & Moranna taking the co-pilot seats, in an urgent effort to try and make evasive manoeuvres. Their ship had a one-of-a-kind deflector shield built especially for warfare, and as it diverted course to move clear of the missiles incoming, what damage it did take was quickly absorbed by the shield. Once out of the way, the majority of enemy fire was now headed straight towards Onix's group. Within a few seconds, twenty-five of his ships at least, were unable to get out of the way in time and succumbed to the full might of Avaloria. These ships either exploded into gulfs of flame and wreckage, which rained down over the ocean or were crippled,

Might & Magic

leaving their smoking carcasses to plummet down into the beach below.

Max advised that their best course of action was to try and steer northwards to avoid any more enemy fire. Onix unfortunately, wasn't afforded such options at his disposal. His ship was no match for anything thrown towards him. It was neither fast enough, nor powerful enough to put up any kind of fight. With his options limited, he had a split-second decision to make. Should he stay and go down with his ship and an empire he no longer believed in? Or should he jump to the side that truly meant something to him now, along with his brother?

At that very moment, as though fate itself made an appearance......'**The Kingslayer**' emerged through the clouds above. Cannon fire suddenly fell silent, as the Avalorian fleet looked up in pure disbelief. A towering slab of darkness covered the sky above, blocking out any daylight in the area. The ship was unlike anything that had graced the skies of any land before. Once the ship had fully descended into a fearsome view for all to see, it paused its advance. Then, as though it came from the very heavens itself, a voice echoed for all below to hear;

'I see that we have all of your undivided attention now. This is the emperor's advisor and captain of '**The Kingslayer**,' Kain. We advise you all to lay down your arms and surrender peacefully. His high exaltedness and the one born of prophecy, emperor Malvik, has come to accept your kingdom as his own, in his pilgrimage for ultimate peace & prosperity for all, under his one rule. You have ten minutes to comply, or we will rain down holy judgment upon you all.'

BY LEE M. COOPER

King Horgath of Avaloria, was listening intently from his palace. He was a man of great renown and tough resolve. He had been on the throne for more than fifty years and built the kingdom up to the mighty and fierce force it was today. The majority of his inner spirit said;

'To hell with them! We will burn them all or die trying!' but deep within, his heart told him to do the sensible thing for his people. This was a force to be reckoned with, and they were not prepared to go to war with such an unexpected force. He sat atop his granite throne and leaned in to speak with his closest advisors.

'My King, this craft of theirs……it is such a size as I have never seen! It has cast the whole city in a great darkness! I fear that if we do not succumb to their demands, no matter how false they may or may not be, then our people may perish…,' said his foreign relations advisor, Myrek.

His chief war advisor Jarfel, then voiced his opinion;

'My lord, there has never been any force that Avaloria has not managed to overcome in the last hundred years. Yes, they may have a fearsome ship of sorts…. but we have the mightiest sea fleet on the planet! We will blow it out of the sky and cast it asunder into the ocean!'

'Hmph,' The King grunted and pondered for a moment, stroking his long grey beard. His wrinkled eyes then looked out from his high window, as he walked across to get a better look at the juggernaut in the sky. After several minutes, he turned to face his advisors in the room and said;

'Patch me through to that ship, I shall give them their answer……'

Might & Magic

Kain paced left and right aboard the bridge of '**The Kingslayer**.' He waited out his long ten minutes as he had promised, to receive their answer. Previous relations between Avaloria and Kavlos in the past had been, strained at best. Each long ago, made a peace treaty to stay away from each other's affairs. Though, they both had a mutual respect for one another. Kavlos had been at the forefront of magical technology and had built its empire over the years becoming successful in many campaigns.

Whereas Avaloria, were second to none on the seas and had developed secret technologies that none could rival. So each nation decided it best, to go their separate ways and rule their own kingdoms in peace. A static line channelled into the ship, Kain stopped and listened intently to the words about to follow.

'Ship of Kavlos, this is the King of Avaloria, King Horgath. Though you have most kindly given us ten minutes to think over your most generous offer….I have made my decision in only seven. AVALORIA SURRENDERS TO NO ONE! LEAST OF ALL, A WARMONGERING WESTERN PIECE OF SELF ENTITLED SCUM, SUCH AS MALVIK!' the King raged.

'PREPARE TO DIE!'

Kain shook his head in disbelief, he turned around and spoke.

'Well my lord, it seems the good King has chosen the path of death.'

Sat in a grand throne, purposely built for him, emperor Malvik leaned in, and a garish smile slowly appeared across his lips.

'So be it….,' he spoke.

BY LEE M. COOPER

Emperor Malvik stood up and walked two paces forward. Lay in front of him, were two orbs raised on pillars. They looked somewhat integral to the ships controls but had no visible buttons. He reached his hands over then and softly placed them down. His now otherworldly eyes flickered and squinted, as his magic essence began to flow through his wretched body, and into the orbs. They started to glow a bright green, and the ship started to make a noise as though it was coming to life, brimming with power.

Max and Thamir aboard the 'Justice,' were still just off to the north and could do nothing now but watch the dreaded standoff.

'Oh my god, what's that ship doing? It looks like it's......beginning to ready for some sort of attack?,' Max shouted in an alarmed voice looking out the viewport.

'That's no ordinary attack, it's Malvik. He is on that ship, and whatever he is about to do………. I feel a great dread for' said Thamir, watching on in a helpless manner.

At the nose of the 'Kingslayer,' great pistons began to process internally, and vents of steam bolted out all over the ship. The engines started to whirl and grunt as though a mighty tornado of death was about to be unleashed. And then, a bright green magic essence began to build at the tip of the nose, as though it was gathering great power to release upon the city below.

'YOU INSOLENT FOOL HORGATH! IF YOU WILL NOT SUPPORT MY CAMPAIGN OF PEACE, THEN IT SHALL BE FORCED UPON YOU!'

Might & Magic

Just as Malvik was about to slam his palms back down on the orbs, and unleash a most devastating blow, it was as though time slowed momentarily. Kain glanced across, sensing something out of place...a noise perhaps, approaching. As he looked out of the window, his eyes widened, and his face turned into a gasp of shock. For coming straight towards the bridge viewport, a battered, flaming imperial ship was headed straight towards them! Kain didn't have time to react, however all he could do was look into the pilot's eyes as he made impact......

......the eyes of **Onix**!

BY LEE M. COOPER

Chapter 16: Battle of The Ancients

As Onix made impact with the bridge of '**The Kingslayer**,' an almighty explosion erupted. It knocked Malvik backwards across the room and shattered the viewport glass. Many onboard staff were immediately sucked out of

Might & Magic

the vortex, pulling them out to their deaths or burnt to a crisp. Kain was knocked unconscious. For any lesser beings stood so close, it would've easily spelt an immediate end. However one of his greatest strengths, was an ability to withstand an unbearable amount of damage, relatively unscathed. Nevertheless, with no one to keep the ship under control, the mighty juggernaut in the sky, began to turn and plummet towards the southern shoreline. It was as though a great catastrophe was about to hit the land below. Bellows of smoke and fire burst forth and flickered from the cockpit's nose.

'Oh my god, that ship……Onix……it's going to cause a tsunami! Take the ship down, we have to try and protect the city!' Max shouted.

He took control of the 'Justice,' along with Thamir and took her down to land on the beach. Their thinking for this, was that if they could combine their powers to put up a magical barrier…it might, just might be enough to keep Avaloria from being flooded. As Jarrel opened up the rear cargo ramp, the crew exited to the beach and stood watching, as **'The Kingslayer'** was falling, diagonally nose first into the water below.

Thamir was first to begin conjuring all his inner might into a force field. He moved his arms and spoke words in an ancient cantation, using all of his spirit, to bring up a fiery wall of pure red energy. Next, Moranna & Jarrel used the magic knowledge they also had at their disposal, casting and feeling the magic flow through their bodies. They too, added a green aura to Thamir's existing barrier. This enlarged and helped enforce the shield tenfold. Finally, Max held both his hands against the barrier and

BY LEE M. COOPER

began to concentrate. His poured all of his magical energy into it, screaming as the force began to take its toll on him. The shield now rose high into the sky and at least five miles or so in every direction.

Malvik's ship finally at this point, crashed into the ocean before them, as expected, causing a tidal wave of epic proportions to head towards the beach.

Halgore then waved his staff in a ritualistic manner, his magic was different, older and more unique. It wasn't the traditional type taught at the Kavlos imperial academy. Halgore raised his staff as it began to emit a bright, white glow, and suddenly.........

'Shhhzzoooommmmm!'

A vast portion of the wave began to break away and was absorbed into a whirlpool of Halgore's creation. The others, though concentrating as they were, couldn't help but be impressed by this natural magic he conjured into the very ocean!

Shadowstorm being the only crew member unable to help, watched on with a nervous disposition. Then, the wave suddenly was upon them. The force field held against the initial force, even though it had been dampened.

Max, Moranna & Jarrel's arms began shaking, their eyes shut tightly as though they were holding the weight of a building on top of them. Even Halgore and Thamir, the two most powerful of the group, visibly struggled. And then, after a moment that felt like an eternity, the water had passed. The crew collapsed in unison to their knees, weakened after such a display of magical prowess.

Might & Magic

'Well……done. That was the most force, I have had to use….in many a year….,' Thamir said huffing & puffing.

'I…..have never…..had to do that….before….,' Moranna said with exhaustion.

'Phew…. we did it. That's the first problem tackled. Now…..what about Kain & Malvik…?' said Max.

The Avalorian fleet had begun opening fire back towards the ships that were left, as explosions erupted once more overhead. The 'Justice' itself, though it had taken a beating from the city's cannons, seemed flyable still. Though, it would need some repairs before she was able to be fully airborne again.

'Max, get to the city. Take Moranna & Jarrel with you. It's the safest place for you both now. Halgore and I will wait here, should they appear. GO, NOW!'

Max nodded at Thamir's words, and grabbed Moranna's hand, as they began to run for the city gates. Jarrel ran shortly behind them, covering their rear with an imperial rifle he took from their ship. Shadowstorm placed his hand on Jarrel's shoulder from behind as he caught up.

'My friend's, if you have any hope at all, of getting through those gates alive, then you will need my assistance.'

Thamir watched them run onwards, turning to Halgore. Both men glanced at one another with a look of uncertainty and worry. The '**Kingslayer**' lay crashed into some rocks, smouldering with plumes of black smoke rising into the air. They couldn't quite tell if there was any movement or not, and then suddenly, the two felt a cold chill gather around them.

BY LEE M. COOPER

'Something vile approaches, I can feel it,' Halgore muttered in a low, grim tone.

'It is him; it is Kain,' Thamir replied.

A storm began to gather above, rumbles and flashes cascaded through the clouds, like ripples of water. And then an immediate hand burst up on the beach, made of sand, grabbing Thamir at his waist pinning him there. Halgore shouted to the sky;

'Show yourselves, cowards!!'

The sky rumbled and flashed aggressively now, pulsing like a heartbeat before a thick bolt of thunder shot down from the heavens, striking a helpless Thamir. The hand exploded around him back into particles of sand, as the jolt sent him flying across the beach. Halgore too, was knocked back by the thunderous blast. As the two lay grounded and gasping for air, a human form emerged from where the bolt had struck, made of pure electricity. Skin then began to gather around the energy, as if from nowhere, settling in the form of Kain.

'I suppose you think you are at an advantage brother...,' Kain said as he slowly walked towards a wounded Thamir.

'How mistaken you are. Why must you continue to interfere with the emperors' plans, after they have been in motion for so long? Do you not want to fulfil your obligation, your reason for being?!'

'Heh...heh....Kain......you misguided fool. If you cannot see what Malvik has become, then you truly are blind. You have veered from your purpose. You have continued to support a maniac posing as a prophecy. And then you march on Avaloria, intent on death and destruction. We

Might & Magic

made a mistake Kain! Onix and I saw the truth, and it is our DESTINY to see our mistakes, put right!'

Kain stared down at his brother, unamused and clearly believing his own actions to be the right ones. Halgore started to come around, looking at the situation at hand, he quickly reached for his staff and quickly pointed it towards Kain. It shot off a ball of white energy directly at him and he was knocked to the floor before he had time to react. His efforts were short lived however, as a sinister laugh echoed through the wind. Halgore mournfully looked at Thamir, before being swallowed by the beach itself!

'Halgore!!' Thamir shouted. But all that appeared from the sandy whirlpool...was Malvik! His sandy form with glowing red eyes, quickly shapeshifted back to his humanoid form, in all his dark and ghastly appearance. He smiled at Thamir, shaking a finger side to side at him, as though in disappointment.

'Thamir, my old teacher. My once loyal advisor. My once loyal servant...... You had not made any error in judgment. This was all as the prophecy foretells.'

'Malvik, I do not know where exactly you began to turn into this demonic lunatic. I blame ourselves, we misread the prophecy. This is all our fault, the KingsGuard........but know this. If it kills me, I WILL put this right! You will not throw Omeria into chaos and darkness!'

Thamir then lit his arms up with serpents of white-hot flame, which ran around his forearms, and then jumped towards Malvik's chest. Malvik, only marginally phased by this, looked at him in annoyance. His fiery, ash smoken sword in one hand, his now menacing looking and warped staff in the other. The orb began to glow atop his staff, before sending out a blast similar to that of Halgore's, towards Thamir. He was able to dodge this however and roll back to his feet. Malvik ran towards him, a mist of black smoke enveloped Malvik, as he clashed swords with Thamir, igniting the blades in an ethereal like aura. Malvik swung and cleaved his blade with great agility, as though someone or something else was moving the weapon for him. Thamir was only just able to keep up, blocking defensively and unable to get on the offensive. The emperor had become all but unrecognisable to Thamir now, he knew something sinister had overcome his very soul just in the way he fought, if nothing else.

After a few minutes of relentless attacks, Malvik had managed to gain the upper hand. The magic projectiles they had been deflecting away from one another, were bouncing into the ocean and causing tidal waves that crashed dramatically across the shoreline rocks. Kain at this point, had managed to regain composure and stood to his feet. He flanked his emperor, as he prepared to give Thamir the killing blow.

'Playtime is over Thamir, it is time to go now and return to whatever force brought you here so long ago,' Malvik confidently snarled at him.

Thamir's armour was smouldering now, from the repeated blows of Malviks evil, dark magic and the cuts of his otherworldly, powerful blade. Defeated and with no other options, Thamir uttered the words;

'I may have failed Omeria in this life Malvik, but I will be back in the next...'

Might & Magic

Malvik laughed as he raised his sword and seconds from a fatal blow, was dragged into the ocean by tentacles of pure water! Kain looked over, confused at what had happened. The water tentacles then whipped back out, grabbing Kain and smashing him face first, into the unforgiving sand. It then wrapped around his feet and with a great speed, swung him around in the air and cast him through the sky.

A look of surprise came over the beaten and bloodied face of Thamir, as he struggled to get to his feet. Then walking out from the tides, came Halgore, as though reborn and looking focused with a glow that radiated around him. He walked over slowly to Thamir, helping him up.

'……it appears you do have some tricks left, Halgore,' he said with a smile.

'Haha, old magic is the most powerful.'

Max, Moranna, Jarrel & Shadowstorm finally came upon the gates to the city of Avaloria. They were surrounded by a great moat, itself patrolled by various battle ships of different sizes. As the city was notoriously defensive, one would have to acquire a permit to lower the gate bridge and enter. As these now effective fugitives, had no prior permission and had come bringing war inadvertently……it was going to be a long stretch to gain entry to say the least.

'Young soldiers of Kavlos, you had best let me lead in this situation,' Shadowstorm said as he pushed his way gently to the front. He walked towards a communication box that visitors were expected to approach, prior to entry into the city. He pushed a button and awaited a reply.

BY LEE M. COOPER

After only a few seconds, an authoritative voice came over the line.

'State your business!'

The four looked at each other, then Shadowstorm readied his reply;

'This is Shadowstorm, formerly of his majesty's guard. I stand with three companions from the empire of Kavlos. We come under direst of circumstances. We come in peace, but we seek to aid the King in the city's defences.

An eerily long silence proceeded, until a high pitch laughter came back across the speaker.

'HAHAHAHAAAAA. Shadowstorm! THE Shadowstorm? The disgrace of Avaloria? You have some guts to show yourself here…. you were banished by royal decree. What use would the King have for an imbecile such as you?'

'You don't understand, we want to help your city defend itself but the best way to do that, is to aim all of your oppressive fire at emperor Malvik and his servant Kain. They are currently locked in battle with two of our friends on the beach. If you let them die now, then you will have lost the only hope of suppressing him!' Max interjected.

There was another long pause, only this time no laughter followed.

'You may enter, but you are to relieve all your weapons at the gate. And if you plan to take advantage of our generosity, we will kill you,' the voice said in a much more serious tone.

A cranking sounded, as mechanical gears and chains whirled to life and the drawbridge began to lower. Once it

Might & Magic

had fully opened, a small battalion of high-tech soldiers armed with rifles marched out to greet the four.

'You will submit your weapons now, if you wish an audience with our King,' the captain said sternly. He looked at Shadowstorm and spat at him. Shadowstorm looked to the floor, in a look of disgrace.

'How dare you show your face here Shadowstorm, if the King doesn't ordain your immediate death this day………it will only be because we have been besieged under this doom you bring to us!' said an infuriated officer.

Once they had handed over their weapons, they were led into the city and the bridge raised back up, sounding an ominous thud once it had fully closed again. Their hands were bound as they were led through the narrow streets of the city. Local citizens watched on and stared at the foreigners with disdain, as though they were common criminals.

'Friendly bunch, aren't they?' Jarrel said with a hint of sarcasm. Shadowstorm answered him back;

'It is not their custom to greet strangers from foreign lands, especially under the circumstances we have arrived in.'

'Are they taking us to speak with their King?' asked Max.

'Oh don't you worry, King Horgath is wise. And he will know just how to deal with you…,' another one of the guards escorting them said rather ominously.

Moranna glared unnervingly at Max, as they continued to be led through the streets and towards the city square. At the foot of the square, lay the golden steps that rose up towards the King's palace. They marched up them and as they approached the top, they couldn't help but notice the

BY LEE M. COOPER

giant statues outside. Max thought they could be former warriors or King's of old from Avaloria's past, either way they looked down upon people eerily as they entered. It sent a slight shiver down his back.

Their path took them through a few more heavily guarded hallways, decorated with paintings of war vessels and ornaments. Not unlike the emperor's own citadel back in Kavlos.

Finally, at the end of the hallway and through the expected grandeur of some grand double doors, this kingdoms King stood waiting to address the four. He was elderly, with a long white beard and was dressed in what appeared to be battle garb. An old looking, battle worn helmet adorned his head as opposed to a crown and his body was dressed in only a slightly more grander looking armour than that of his soldiers. The banner of his city draped over his cloak, which hung over one of his shoulders. He was a stark contrast to King's Moranna, Jarrel and Max had seen or heard of in the past.

The King stared at the four, in a distrustful manner. He seemed regularly active and preferred to get his hands dirty himself, so to speak. Horgath approached them as they stood in a line, hands cuffed and wondering just how this was about to play out. The King didn't show much of an interest in the Kavlosian's, but upon looking at Shadowstorm who was clearly a former native of the city, his interest peaked somewhat. His pale grey eyes stared deep into his former captains.'

Might & Magic

'Shadowstorm, when last we spoke, as I remember, you were banished under pain of death, should you return. Tell me, are you that eager to die?'

'Your highness,' Moranna butted in gaining the King's scornful look of attention.

'If you please, Shadowstorm is only here at our behest. He was noble enough to join our fight against the tyranny of our emperor. He fought with great valiance and skill in our kingdom's Knightfall tournament. He has also proved his worth in helping us escape Kavlos, in the hope of rallying your aid to stop emperor Malvik, before something dreadful happens to this city.'

'Oh? Really. Well now that is interesting. Once upon a time, Shadowstorm here was amongst my finest men. However he failed to protect the innocent, and in our custom, we banish the weak. It is how we have survived and thrived so long in the world. And now he comes back with a rag-tag group of ex-communicated kavlosian soldiers.'

The King looked Moranna up and down, then leaned into her ear.

'Tell me, if you were me....what would you do? Would you protect your people, or would you take the word of a banished wretch and the army he brings with him?'

'Listen, I know it must seem bad, but I warn you now, if you ignore our warning then this city WILL suffer the consequences. I say this not as an enemy, but as a friend,' she replied in her most serious tone.

'Hmph. And what proof do you have, that you do come as a friend? That you are not a part of your emperor's plot

BY LEE M. COOPER

to kill us all?' the King asked walking back to be seated on his throne.

'Sir! Report!' a soldier chimed in over the Kings radio com.

'Proceed...'

'My King, we have now managed to clear the skies of enemy ships, and any that weren't shot down, have fled back to the Kingdom of Kavlos.'

The King smiled;

'Very good captain, very good,' he replied.

'Errr my King, there is.... just one small issue,' the soldier began to sound slightly panicked on the other side of the radio.

'What is it?'

'There are two battered & bloodied mage looking individuals at the gate, ordering admittance. Should we let them in my lord?'

The King looked up at the four in handcuffs.

'Well, what do you think? Are these friends of yours?'

Max looked at the others by his side, who returned his look of confusion and uncertainty.

'Well, that depends your highness.......,' Max replied.

Fifteen minutes earlier

Thamir laughed at Halgore.

'You do continue to surprise me, I thought you was dead,' Thamir said with a look of mixed joy and confusion as he lay knelt on the beach. Halgore smiled at him, then extended his hand to help him up.

Might & Magic

'I do not know how long my magic can hold him for, but I suspect it won't be long. We must hurry and catch up with the others' a tired Halgore advised, as they both began to stagger along the beach, following their companions' footsteps towards Avaloria. As they departed the beach, the ocean began to bubble and emit a strange glow.

The two ancient mages staggered through the sandy pathway, past trees and bushes as they tracked the footsteps of their comrades. After a short trek, they came out from the last coverages of flora & fauna, revealing an iconic view of Avaloria and its patrolling forces.

'Let us hope the others arrived safely and can manage to convince the King to help us,' mused Thamir.

As the two strode forward from the foliage, a hand fell on eithers shoulder and they quickly turned ready to attack….

'ONIX?! My brother, but how? I thought you were dead?' Thamir happily said with joy in his voice.

'I am not so easily defeated brother; I am only sorry I could not get away sooner.'

'Do not worry Onix, you brought us time. That is more valuable than anything I could have asked of you.'

Halgore, also looked overjoyed that the two brothers had reunited.

'Ha! What a sight to see. I am glad you are ok Onix, listen you two go ahead. I will follow you shortly, I just want to make sure you have the time you need, should Malvik make a re-appearance!'

BY LEE M. COOPER

'Halgore, you cannot face him alone....if he does come back he will kill you!' Onix said, trying to appeal to his better judgment.

'Do not worry about me, remember I have a long history with him. My magic may not be as strong as it once was, but it is still strong enough! I will be ok, now go....you must help the others!.'

Thamir & Onix looked at each other with concern, then turned back to Halgore. They nodded in anxious agreement, and each placed a hand on his shoulder in great respect, before moving onwards to the city. Halgore gave a gentle smile, and then turned to look behind him. He could see nothing but the overgrowing leaves of the great surrounding trees, he could hear nothing but the swaying of them in the now gentle breeze. Nevertheless, he squeezed and gripped his staff tightly and patted down his still soaking robes. Minutes passed, but still........nothing, nothing but silence. Halgore didn't like this, it was quiet, too quiet. He slowly walked his way through the foliage, back the way he had come. Moving the branches gently out of his path with his staff........ he stopped. A voice echoed to him through the trees, and so he cautiously walked towards where it was coming from. He was aware of course, that he was probably walking into a trap, but the voice sounded like that of a child.

He came upon a clearing, as he stepped slowly towards what appeared to be the source of the voice.....a small child. A young girl to be exact, no older than seven or eight at the most.

Might & Magic

'Sniff...sniff.......daddy, daddy where are you?,' said the little girl. She was sat down, dressed in rags and looking very distressed. Halgore took back his staff from an offensive position, a look of kindness came across his face as he leaned down to speak to the lost, crying girl.

'Are you ok young one? My name is Halgore, please don't be afraid I am here to help. Have you lost your father?

'Sniff...sniff......Yes, he went over there to gather wood for our fire. But that was a long time ago and he told me to wait here....,' said the upset little girl.

Halgore looked up, walking over towards the direction the little girl pointed. Just as he did, he gasped.....breathless and unable to speak! He looked down to see an orb emerging through his chest.....burning white hot, as he dropped to his knees. He turned to look at the little girl, who smiled sadistically before fading away into smokey ash. A familiar voice spoke to him over his shoulder, as a sickening grin appeared;

'Halgore my old friend heh heh heh. I thought after all these years, you would know better than to wander off alone, you fool.'

Halgore's body was then thrown to the ground, as the white-hot orb retracted from his back. He lay there........ finally dead after so many long years, with only a look of shock left upon his withered, old face and a burnt hole through his smoking chest.

'One down.......Avaloria left to go...... ha ha ha,' Malvik laughed to himself with a twisted, sick purpose as he stamped his staff down on the ground.

BY LEE M. COOPER

He looked through the trees, and there stood waiting, was his next target. Avaloria...

Might & Magic

Chapter 17: The Final Stand

King Horgath asked his captain, what these two 'mages,' looked like exactly.

'Erm, well my King. They claim to be party members of your current company. They are wearing some kind of ancient looking armour. One is clad in Green, the other in red,' said the captain on the other end of the radio.

'Thamir and….Onix? Could he have somehow survived?' Max wondered to himself.

BY LEE M. COOPER

'Yes! They are our comrades. They join our fight to stop the crazed emperor' Moranna said jumping out of line and waving her cuffed hands about, as though trying to explain with them.

'Your highness, you must let them through. They are perhaps your best hope now to save your city!' Jarrel also shouted, trying to build on Moranna's argument.

The King looked at them both, still untrusting but having mulled it over in his head now for some time.

'Send them in but be careful! If they are mages of old, then they are extremely dangerous!'

After a couple of minutes, the throne room doors swung open and Thamir & Onix were marched in by a small platoon of armed guards. The guards circled behind them, their guns pointed towards their backs, not realising that bullets had no effect on them. The two former KingsGuard members glanced across the room to their companions, before addressing the King himself.

'Good King Horgath, I believe you may already have been debriefed on how dangerous the situation here is. I believe by the fact you are still stood here, that you are not treating this with the urgency it requires,' Onix said in a serious tone.

Thamir stepped forward, easily breaking the hand cuffs he was in, like they were mere blades of grass.

'We must not prattle any longer! The real enemy will be upon your gates very soon, I am certain of it!'

King Horgath laughed mockingly.

'Ha ha. Silence! I am King of these lands, and I will decide how to rule as I see fit!'

Might & Magic

Max, Jarrel & Moranna looked at each other in frustration, knowing they were fighting a losing battle. It was now clear, there was only one way this King would believe anyone, and the three feared that time was almost upon them.

'For now, throw them all in the brig!' King Horgath ordered, in a commanding voice.

'You're making a huge mistake King Horgath!' Thamir shouted, with a light of anger in his eyes.

As the guards grabbed the newly appointed prisoners' arms, to take them out of the throne room, a blood curdling scream echoed over the King's coms radio.

'Captain….captain report!,' Horgath ordered immediately.

No reply came, only gunfire and the sound of explosions. And then a reply finally came;

'King Horgath. This is emperor Malvik of Kavlos, and I believe you are holding an audience with several traitors to the crown. I am done with pleading with you to surrender your city, or your present company. However, if you could please pass a message on for me. Tell them, their good friend Halgore won't be joining them…..ever again haha. Your city will now burn, along with you in it. None shall prevent me from fulfilling my destiny!'

Malvik then cut off the airwave. Explosions were then heard outside as guards came rushing in.

'My King! My King! We are under attack. I think its emperor Malvik, but….but…he's changed…..somehow………like a demon!'

BY LEE M. COOPER

King Horgath looked around the room furiously then stormed towards the door, unsheathing his sword, he bellowed;

'Unchain the captors! We fight with all the will of Avaloria, we smite this demon once and for all!'

Shadowstorm stood proudly to attention, as though he had been given an order from years ago when he was still in service. A soldier quickly walked amongst them, unlocking their handcuffs and passing their weapons back to them. Shadowstorm held his sword in both of his hands, he stroked the blade with one hand, and it came to life in a wreath of purple flame. They all walked back into the hallway and followed the King down to the exit. They could see the daylight of the sky breaking through at the end, but also flickers of fire and black smoke.

As the company stood outside, they observed the carnage that was occurring below in the city. One man, Malvik, was single handedly wiping the populace out. His dark, charred, smoking, evil visage was cleaving through innocent people. He severed heads from bodies and raised buildings into flame and ruin with the mere flick of his hand. He had truly given over his soul to the depths of hell or some other underworldly entity.

The King charged thoughtlessly in anger, towards the demonic presence cutting its way through the streets. The King was old yet foolhardy. He believed in his many years of rule, that he was somewhat undefeatable in battle. However as he ran towards Malvik, sword raised he screamed as though in a war cry;

Might & Magic

'DIE DEMON, GO BACK TO THE DEPTHS OF HELL FROM WHENCE YOU CAME!!!'

He shouted, as he was about to bring his blade down. Though it would come at a foolish cost. Malvik held out his long spindly fingers, and caught the blade effortlessly, turning it into ash within seconds. Horgath looked stunned, as his sword disintegrated in his very hands. His look then turned to one of horror, as Malvik lifted him by his throat and opening his fiery demonic like mouth, emitted a breath of hellish flame.

Thamir, Onix & the rest of the company along with royal guards loyal to the King, stared down at the top of the stairs, as they watched the long ruling King turn into ash.

'Jarrel, Moranna, Max you three get to the guns on the walls. Alone I fear they will be powerless against Malvik, but if you can imbue them with magic essence, it will increase the effect tenfold and may just give us the edge that we need! Shadowstorm, help get the people to safety. Onix & I will handle Malvik....'

Max nodded and ran towards the city stairs to get a higher vantage point on the guns. Moranna and Jarrel did the same, albeit in different directions. Onix and Thamir slowly descended the stairs, their hands poised in a fighting stance, each alight with their respective elemental powers. Onix's eyes glowed a bright green, as he summoned the earth beneath Malvik to shake. Great vines came up from the ground and wrapped around the once proud man of prophecy. Malvik fell to his knees, grunting through his now sharp fang like teeth. His pale grey, stretched skin of his face, now pulsing with thick bluey, green veins underneath in anger. His once long silver like

BY LEE M. COOPER

fine hair, smoked like ashen tentacles that had come to life.

'What the hell have you become' Onix said in disgust, using all of his strength and might to keep Malvik down.

Thamir followed up his brothers' attack, he began to run, and jumping off of the side of a nearby building, his feet left a trail of fire burning. He charged his fist with the hottest fire he could muster, his eyes aflame as they once were in days of old, as he delivered a powerful fiery punch straight to his face.

'AAAARRRGGGHHHHHHH!'

Malvik reeled in pain as his head smashed into the ground. He lifted his face up and spat what would once be blood but was now a thick, black liquid. Malvik shook his arms and stamped his staff on the ground, the orb that sat atop it began to come to life with a white glow. It burnt the vines from his arms and freed him back up to his feet. He snarled and grunted like a wild beast, furious that anyone had disrespected him in such a manner or had tried to stop his self-proclaimed campaign of peace! This of course, had become nothing more than a warped dream in his already bent, and twisted mind. Next to nothing was left now of the old Malvik. All that remained, was whatever demonic force had possessed him through the book of rebirth that he carried. A book he found so long ago and misunderstood, to terrible consequences.

He shot a blast of white energy from his staff, hitting Thamir back into a wall and smashed through it with full force. A blow that would certainly kill a lesser being. As Onix tried to fire a great whirlwind from his hands at

Might & Magic

Malvik, he managed to deflect it with his staff. The demonic emperor then brought about his fiery, smoking sword to cut off his head! Onix managed to dodge & roll out of the way but was not quick enough to avoid his next imminent strike.

A ball of green energy, wrapped around a cannon ball suddenly smashed into Malvik's chest at high velocity. It had come from Max, high above on the city walls who had managed to man one of the wall cannons, much to his joy. Malvik's eyes burned a ferocious red, his body though still lay on the ground, limp.

'Another!' cried Moranna from another nearby post, high on the wall.

'I've got this, guys Prepare to watch the killing blow that will make me, Jarrel 'the conqueror,' when I return home.'

Jarrel loaded and pointed a wall mounted turret directly towards Malvik and placed his hands on the cannon. He poured everything he had into it, all his essence, his strength and his desire to finish off the once mighty emperor, as he fired off the highly explosive shot! The cannon ball exited in a giant ball of pulsing power, picking up speed by the second as it fired. Though to Malvik, he was able to watch its approach towards him in fractions of a second. His mind was able to slow down time itself. He knew himself; he had been hasty and overconfident before. That was about to change. Malvik lifted his right arm, slowing down the ball of blazing, green energy and with a twist of his wrist....sent the shot hurtling back towards Jarrel.

BY LEE M. COOPER

Jarrel's eyes widened in shock as he saw the ball stop, and swoop around to head back towards him! Max shouted out, as he watched on in horror.

'JARREELLLLLLLLLL!!!!!'

His screams to his best friend fell on deaf ears, however. There was not enough time in the world it seemed, to stop what was about to happen. Moranna looked on in horror, then dropped to her knees. An explosion of green aura hit Jarrel, blowing out a chunk of the city wall. His death was immediate, painless. Nothing was left once the green mist disappeared on the breeze, but a smouldering cavity where he once stood. Moranna screamed in anger, she unsheathed her sword and leaped from the wall, down towards Malvik. As she descended, her eyes were ablaze with magical power and her sword came to life with the same glow.

Malvik managed to get to his feet by this point, he raised his staff as he began to conjur a spell to destroy her effortlessly. Just then, a glowing green katana blade appeared from his side, cutting through the staff to Malvik's surprise. It cleaved it clean in two, the orb cracking and shattering into tiny pieces of glass to the floor. The evil emperor's face distorted in shock.

'NO! How can this be? There is no power on Omeria that can stop me!' he shouted.

Moranna then landed her intended piercing strike, straight into Malvik's chest, as he screamed in agony, falling to his knees. Max then also struck him, plunging his sword into his back.

'This is for Jarrel, you monster!'

Might & Magic

'AAARRGGHHHHHHHHHH, HOW……DARE……,' he tried to speak, the sound of his thick, black blood gurgling in his throat.

Still, Malvik tried to defy his death. His knees shook, as he tried to stand, he picked up his sword and raised it above his head. Onix and Thamir jumped to their aid, combining their powers to create a vortex of white-hot fire around the mad villain. Malvik, his warped, devilish armour beginning to melt as his face burned still, refused to die!

And then, with one last ditch effort attempt, Max grabbed the vile sword from Malvik's hand and thrust it through his throat. The four stood back, as Malvik gasped his last breath. The vortex turned a purple colour as it finally died down, leaving his smokey, ruined corpse behind. He fell forward, face down onto the floor…..Malvik was finally defeated.

Shadowstorm was helping direct civilians to the nearest exit's, commanding the guards as he once did and feeling a familiar sense of pride as he did so. He stopped across the way, as he looked on to see the emperor finally fall.

As Max, Moranna, Onix & Thamir gathered around the former emperor's corpse, they looked on in amazement as his original appearance began to come back. His once possessed, black armour now began to return to its original silver, gleaming state. His face returned from a pale, distorted grim visage to his once handsome, human form. Whatever had possessed him had now left his body.

'The city is now safe, though the toll here today has been a heavy one,' said Onix as he surveyed the fire and bodies littered around him.'

BY LEE M. COOPER

Max fell to one knee, shedding a tear. Emotion overcame him as he thought about his friend that lost his life. About Halgore who had given his, to buy them time. Moranna crouched and hugged him, as he returned her embrace.

Overhead, the clouds dispersed, as the sun began to shine through once more. As though a sign of the passing evil had finally left the land. Shadowstorm walked over to the group and bent his knee before them.

'My friends! I cannot thank you enough for destroying this evil and saving these lands. I understand that you have lost friends here today, but your strength is unlike anything I have seen. The kingdom of Avaloria owes you a great debt this day.'

Max wiped his eyes and stood to his feet, holding his ribs in pain.

'Shadowstorm, it has been a great honour to have met you. And I'm sure Jarrel and Halgore are smiling somewhere, their deaths will not have been in vain. They understood what their fight was against and were ready to accept the consequences. We must give them, and the other casualties here a proper burial of some kind.'

'You have all indeed fought a near impossible fight this day,' said Onix.

'However, Thamir and I must return to Kavlos shortly, once the ship is repaired. The city is currently without leadership beyond temporary acting generals, and we must rectify that as soon as possible. The kingdom is without a crown, and so a public vote must now happen to elect a new leader, under Kavlosian law'

Might & Magic

'Max, Moranna you should stay here a while. You have much to grieve over and I am sure Shadowstorm would welcome your help here for a while,' added Thamir.

'Avaloria will of course aid you with whatever you need, though our King has fallen this day, and our city will need to grieve for him when the time is right,' said the royal captain.

'Shadowstorm, we have judged you unfairly and for your bravery in the face of adversity today, I would like to extend an offer with humblest apologies and welcome you back.... should you wish to honour us with your services once more'?

Shadowstorm nodded in acceptance;

'Thank you, captain. If you please, once we have helped the wounded here, our friends could do with some repairs on their ship. It would only require some small adjustments, but it lies on the beach, currently out of commission.'

'Of course, I shall get our best mechanics on it right away, it's the least we can do,' the captain then departed to make the necessary arrangements without delay, grabbing two of his men to follow.

Thamir & Onix thanked Shadowstorm, then looked back at the body of their fallen enemy. After so long, their misread prophecy had finally come to an end in Malvik. Though they couldn't help but wonder, where did this demonic power come from? And if this happened once, could it stand to reason that it could happen again? Once they had made suitable arrangements in Kavlos, they knew that the answers they seeked, would lie in only one place……the Temple of Creation.

BY LEE M. COOPER

Might & Magic

Epilogue

Avaloria. Kavlos. It was fortunate that within Omeria, only these two great kingdoms suffered any kind of tyranny and chaos. The world came terrifyingly close to falling into darkness just three weeks prior.

In Avaloria, the days that followed Malvik's attempted takeover were dark. However the avalorian's were a proud and strong people, they pulled together to clear up what destruction remained. The wounded and the dead were treated and buried accordingly, and people had already started to re-build around the affected areas of the city.

Shadowstorm stood overlooking the cities workers hammering and grafting away, from the balcony of the royal palace. His former, rusted armour had now been replaced by a brand-new shining, royal guards' suit of armour. He watched on proudly, he felt a sense of belonging once more, to the duty that previously meant so much to him. In many ways, it was what he lived for. As he turned to walk back through the halls of the former King Horgath's palace, at the far end now stood a statue to commemorate him. Shadowstorm remembered his brashness, his boldness, his leadership but also his overconfidence which ultimately led to his downfall. The future now would be the dawning on a new era. Beyond the royal throne room doors, lay an empty throne. The King had a son, who by royal decree, the throne would usually fall to. In this instance however, his son was not yet of age, being only ten years old.

Therefore, the next appropriate course of action, would be to issue an acting steward, until such a time as the next in line was ready to rule.

'Sir, sorry to interrupt. However, we have reports that an unauthorised ship has just come into view, off the western shore. Your orders sir?'

'AH! Captain Verrick, a fine report. Send out a small welcoming party, if they are friend then show them food and accommodation, after their long journey. If they are not, then make sure to point them in the right direction, if

Might & Magic

you catch my meaning captain!' Shadowstorm said in a jolly, yet authoritative manner.

'Very good, Steward Shadowstorm, sir.'

The captain bowed gracefully before exiting the room to action his orders, and Shadowstorm climbed the four golden steps and turned to sit on the throne. He had been elected within a mere few days following the attack, as a suitable steward to lead the city, and the Kingdom in the interim. This was the honour of his life, and he sat pondering to himself, if this moment came via fate, or was it pure luck? In any case, he made a promise to himself and his people, that he would act with honour, integrity and try not to make the same mistakes of King Horgath. Avaloria would be an amenable and safe kingdom henceforth, he had also started to see arrangements made with Kavlos and had even reached out to the far western continents, in the hopes of making new peace treaties.

It was a wake-up call to him, that the threats of the world lie in more than just invading armies or corrupt politicians. But also ancient evils the world did not yet fully understand. However, he would see to it that they would collaborate with the best historians and magic users in the world, to improve their defences.

That also meant regular meetings with the newly formed '**Omerian council of magic.**' It was formed in the wake of the recent attacks and consisted of the most powerful magic practitioners in the world. The backbone of which were Thamir and Onix, being that they were the oldest now known.

Shadowstorm looked out of a nearby window, the sky was blue, and the day was a clear one. He smiled, though this soon turned into a look of slight confusion. He stood up and walked over to the window ledge, to get a better view. Something seemed out of place, as on the far distant horizon, a storm cloud was beginning to gather over the ocean.

Meanwhile, in Kavlos…

Max had just finished eating some of his mother's home-made beef stew.

'Well mum, you haven't lost your touch. That was delicious as always, thank you' he said, wiping his mouth clean.

'Oh, my pleasure hun. It was your fathers favourite too. It's just so nice to have you back home for a little while. After all, you need to rest. You've been through quite the journey.'

'Ha, thanks mum. You know me though, always on the lookout for the next one!'

'Well, maybe your next adventure could be with that nice lady friend of yours…. what was her name again?'

'Moranna, mum. And no, we aren't like that. She's a work colleague that's all,' Max said, rolling his eyes as though he'd been asked the same question a thousand times.

'Oh, well that's a pity. She seems very lovely. So, how long do you plan on staying?' Martha asked.

'Well the coronation of the new grand ruler is in two days, so I thought I might stick around for that and then…who knows. Wherever the empire sends me I guess?'

Might & Magic

Later that day, Max was sat in the same pub with Moranna, that they were in weeks ago. They hadn't had a chance to properly sit and talk since the incident happened. They each sat cradling a drink, a spare one sat adjacent to them. They each tapped their cups against the third.

'For Jarrel and Halgore. Two very different friends, but equally as honourable' Max sombrely said.

'It was my fault Jarrel isn't here now, sat with us...I should've gotten him out of the way or, or something...'

'Hey, now you mustn't start blaming yourself. I was there too remember, there wasn't a thing you could've done differently. We were all up against a force unlike anything anyone has ever seen,' Moranna caressed his hand over the table trying to reassure him.

'Thanks Moranna,' he smiled.

'You know, I remember when we were kids. He would always get me in trouble, edging me on to things and trying to see who could make the biggest explosion in my back garden. Mum always used to say, I don't want you hanging around with that boy anymore, he's bad news!'

Max's smile grew as his mind took him back to his childhood, before he quickly returned.

'You're a great friend, Moranna. What will you do now?

'Well, the interim grand ruler has assigned me a mission. After the coronation, I'm to lead a team to the western continent, to Mariva to escort Shadowstorm and his men, in discussing a unified peace treaty.'

'Wow, that is an incredible assignment. And I can't think of a better person for the job. Well, if you ever need another member for your team.....,' Max grinned.

BY LEE M. COOPER

'Oh don't worry. I am sure there will be plenty of opportunities in this new world we are building, Max. I have no doubt you will go on to do remarkable things yourself.'

'Ha, we shall see. I just can't help but feel a sense of lingering dread over me though. No one has seen or heard from Kain since the attack on Avaloria, and I'm fairly sure a mage as powerful as him isn't dead…. not yet anyway'

She fixed her eyes on his, as though in a worrying agreement.

'Max, I have the same feeling. I don't think, if he IS still alive, that he would be foolish enough to come back to Kavlos. Nor do I think he would settle in Avaloria's lands. It's part of the reason I'm so eager to go to Mariva, not just to sign the treaties but I also want to leave a small scouting party there. If he is alive and there, my men will find him, I'm sure.'

Max nodded, adding;

'Well if that does turn out to be the case, just be careful. He was always powerful and dangerous, but now he's unhinged too. I just hope for all our sake's, that Halgore managed to finish him off that day.'

Three days later, The Temple of Creation…

Thamir and Onix both now stood outside the entrance to their once long lived home. It still appeared decrepit from the outside, just as they remembered it.

Might & Magic

'This place never seems to change brother,' Thamir said as he looked over the crumbling, desert red ruins of the secret temple.

'Indeed, though it now just torments my mind that this is the place that we made the gravest of mistakes,' returned Onix.

He waved his hand over the false, bricked up entrance, creating a portal through which they both stepped through.

'Remember brother, that is why we are here. To right our wrongs and find out where exactly we were deceived. The magic that Malvik wielded in the end, was otherworldly and it was nothing we taught him...'

Thamir puckered his lips together, into a soft frown of sorts. The two were now stood in the hall of the true temple, in all its former glory. It was as though they had only been away for a moment, and everything was exactly as they had left it.

The torches were still ablaze on the walls, in their strange colours. The three thrones still lay in their respective places, harkening back to earlier times.... less complicated times. Onix graced his hand along his former throne, as memories flooded back to him of the many years, they lay in wait for the one of prophecy to find them.

He looked over to the third throne, Kain's throne. Onix began to ponder, deep in thought.

'Still, no sign or word from Kain?' he asked.

Thamir shook his head disappointingly.

'No, but like you……I do not feel as though he has yet left this world. Something tells me we haven't heard the last of him, Onix.'

Thamir then walked towards where the tile had turned upon his earlier investigations, showing the terrible vision of destruction and fire.

'Here brother, here is where I discovered a terrible truth,' he said.

Onix looked up and began to walk over to him from the other side of the room. He placed his hands on his hips and squinted his eyes, as he looked back and re-read the scriptures along the wall. He had looked these over hundreds of times in his life, but now the ending tile had flipped to show this now alternative ending. As he reached the end, he moved his lips around as though deep in thought.

'Hmmm…' he mumbled, as he placed his hand on the tile…..and flipped it to the middle. Behind the sides of the tile, he felt a gentle breeze.

'Thamir, come….look at this. Theres an airflow coming from behind the wall.'

'A passage of sorts, perhaps? he replied.

Onix reached his hand behind, he felt something strong, as though made of steel. He placed his hand around it and gave it a yank! Suddenly a 'Chlichuk' noise sounded, followed by the grumbling of heavy stone moving.

They both stood back as the solid stone wall beside the last tile, began to suddenly break into a door shape, and slowly swing open as it kicked up centuries of settled dust. When it finally opened fully, Thamir and Onix looked at

Might & Magic

one another with surprised concern. Beyond the secret door, lay a spiralling stairwell downwards, enveloped in sheer darkness.

'Well brother, it seems after all this time......this temple is still full of surprises. What could this mean?' Onix curiously asked.

'I am not sure, but maybe it will lead to the answers we are looking for.'

Thamir held out his right hand and emitted a small ball of fire, to illuminate the passageway down. They cautiously made their descent down, into the mysterious depths of the Temple. After around ten minutes, a purple glow flickered along the walls and Thamir looked behind him at his mage brother, before dampening his own flame.

Just around the corner, they at last came to the bottom of the stairwell. Cobwebs and a distinct smell of something incredibly old, littered the depths here. The odd coloured purple light, which emanated from two exceptionally large braziers, danced along an altar of sorts. As the two ancient mages slowly stepped towards it, they tried to decipher its design.

Evidently and immediately upon looking at the altar......it stank of evil and anger and hatred. Long fangs protruded up & downwards, made from bone, in the shape of some kind of long dead beast. Its eye holes were inhabited by glowing red crystals, the two mages sensed a very ancient power coming from it. Within the mouth of the skeletal creature, was a small marble tablet. And on that, lay a book besides another book shaped indentation.

'What in the name of all that is holy, is this shrine of evil?' Onix asked, in a disgusted and shocked tone.

BY LEE M. COOPER

'I have no idea brother'

Thamir rubbed his hand slowly over the empty indentation. His head suddenly pounded with a sensation such as he had never felt before. He stepped back, holding his head in pain as he gasped.

'Thamir, are you alright!?' said Onix, rushing to his aid and holding him by the shoulders.

'Argh….ye….yes….yes I think so. Something just hit my mind, like….a voice. It sounded dark……evil and yet……familiar at the same time.'

Onix looking at his brother with concern, glanced over to the book that was sat beside the empty slot. He stepped over and picked it up. The book looked to be a journal of some kind, covered in dust, he brushed his hand over the front and blew away the cobwebs. He opened the cover and turned to the first page.

'Thamir……this appears to be a diary of some sort. Listen……'

'Year of Kavlos four hundred and fifty-seven, day three of my training. The three mages Thamir, Onix and Kain have taken me in and believe me to be some kind of prophesised being. Can it be mere coincidence that I have stumbled upon here? Or is it destiny? They say I am to bring about an everlasting peace across the world……I always knew I was destined for something greater than the village, back home. I know I have something deep inside of me that is calling…. calling to get out.'

Onix began to skim read, brushing some pages across.

'Year of Kavlos four hundred and fifty-eight, day five hundred and ten of my training. My progress is coming

Might & Magic

along nicely. I now am able to conjur and cast a variety of different magics, both defensive and offensively. My tutors believe it won't take long before we are ready to leave and move on to the next step, in my destiny.

'Year of Kavlos four hundred and fifty-eight, day six hundred and forty-five. Whilst my masters were meditating, a voice appeared to me in my head. It spoke to me, one moment I remember standing looking at the scriptures on the wall and the next, I found myself pulled towards this….this altar. I found a book within its mouth, at least I think you could call it that. I know not what the creature was, but as I leaned in to pick up the book, it's red eyes glowed. The voice in my head, it kept saying 'the prophecy lies within, the prophecy lies within.' The book is written in a language I would normally scarcely understand, but somehow the voice in my head reads the pages to me. It makes more sense now; I understand now. The **Book of Rebirth** was what it said on the cover.

As I turned the pages, a light opened to me. It showed me what I must do to fulfil my destiny. I feel….power…power like never before. I see a figure, in a distant realm somewhere, I cannot make it out, but the figure is laced in shadow and flame.

It has a prisoner…… the prisoner cries out in pain….reaching……reaching through bars of ashen fire…..'Star……star….Heart,' I think the voice cries. What does this mean? I do not know; however I think the strength this entity imbues me with, will hasten my training. I am confident it will show me the way, but I must keep it secret. The voice tells me that if anyone should find the book and what lies within its pages, that it's power will

BY LEE M. COOPER

disappear. The prisoner, this 'Starheart,' I can only imagine must be a great evil of some sort. Alas, there will be naught to worry about. I know what I must do, it will help me to suppress the evil's that I will face. All I must do now, is be patient and let the spirit guide me.

Malvik'

As Onix finished reading the last passage, he looked up in horror to Thamir.

'Brother……this is the power that must have possessed Malvik. How were we blind to see this for so long? What could this mean?'

'I……know not Onix. All I know is that if this **'Book of Rebirth'** still remains in Omeria somewhere….then, there is a chance it may fall into the wrong hands once more. It would seem Malvik was but the first to read this.'

'Brother, we must locate this book at all costs!' Thamir said in a gravely sounding, low tone, to which Onix gestured in agreement.

Later that day, back in the capital city of Kavlos. A new grand ruler had been elected. This turned out to be a former general in the King's personal guard. Lady Sariah, had been a good hearted yet fierce warrior, loyal to the late King. She was respected, loved and admired by all who knew or served with her. Sariah was dedicated to Kavlos, and in a public election, had won by a landslide to be the next acting ruler. Around forty-five years of age, she always wore beautifully designed, long robes laced with golden emblems and eye-catching designs. The beginning of her new reign saw her in clothes no dissimilar, as she sat on the throne, in the late King's

Might & Magic

palace. As evening fell, she found herself wondering around the library in the palace, studying the multitude of different topics the King had collected.

'My lady, is there anything you require this evening?,' asked one of the servants who had just walked in to check on her, as part of their evening rounds.

'Oh, thank you. I was just browsing the library. I never really had time to study anything in here when I served his highness. I do miss him. Acting as the new ruler here will take some getting used to, but in here, amongst these books...I almost feel like a part of him is still here.'

'I understand my lady'

'I...do have one question however'

'Of course, what is it?'

'Since Malvik died, what has become of the citadel? Has anyone entered since?

'Ah, a good question my ladyship. Well since we heard of his death and the new leadership has been established, we had the royal guard cordon it off. No one has entered since. Would you wish to revisit it soon my lady?

'I see. Yes, yes maybe tomorrow I will pay it a visit...see what we can do with the place. Perhaps it could stand as a new monument of sorts, to the history of the royal line, for even the public to be able to visit.'

'Very good my lady, until tomorrow then,' said the servant as he bowed before leaving the room and closing the doors.

Lady Sariah smiled, as she thought about the future. It wasn't set in stone, yet the beautiful setting sun and the early rising of a full moon somehow signified to her, that a new, better dawn was coming.

BY LEE M. COOPER

The Emperor's Citadel, Kavlos...

As the moon slowly began to arise, it felt so large this night that it almost cast a shadow on the now empty and derelict citadel, that once housed emperor Malvik for so many years. High up in the former emperor's throne room, a breeze fluttered leaves in through the balcony. And by the side of the balcony, still lay a table. Upon it, was the **Book of Rebirth**.

It lay there....silent.....until suddenly, the lid swung open on its own and the pages began to turn. It landed on one particular page.....and then a bright, red light beamed out of it, amongst the sound of an eery whisper.......'**Star**.....**Heart!**'

Might & Magic

Printed in Great Britain
by Amazon